# The Dance of the Deep-Blue Scorpion

THE ARAB LIST

# The Dance of the Deep-Blue Scorpion

## AKRAM MUSALLAM

TRANSLATED BY SAWAD HUSSAIN

LONDON NEW YORK CALCUTTA

SERIES EDITOR

**Hosam Aboul-Ela**


**Seagull Books, 2021**

Originally published as *Sirat al-'akrab alladhi yatasabbab 'araqan*, 2008
© Akram Musallam, 2008

First published in English translation by Seagull Books, 2021
English translation © Sawad Hussain, 2021

ISBN   978 0 8574 2 893 6

**British Library Cataloguing-in-Publication Data**
A catalogue record for this book is available from the British Library

Typeset by Seagull Books, Calcutta, India
Printed and bound in the USA by Integrated Books International

To those who have lost their limbs in war,
or to medical oversight or a fault of history . . .
or even an old, rusty nail!

END OF 1988

## SCORPION'S BIRTH

We were teenagers. She came to me; to the 'dance hall' at the start of the night; suddenly she came to me, and after a brief chat, she said she had come to show me her freshly tattooed scorpion, just below her spine.

Faded blue jeans and a brick-red blouse revealing a strip of flesh atop her navel is what she had on. We sat on the edge of the platform designated for the band in the dance hall—where I would sleep on a modest mattress. She swivelled round and hunched forward, trying to show off the tattoo, her fingertips tugging at her jeans. I couldn't see much, which she understood, so she loosened her jeans to reveal a small cobalt-blue scorpion lying on a body the colour of the shore; a body that had much to say, a body bubbling with recklessness.

I stroked the scorpion, spending some time doing so, a mysterious puzzle inviting more and yet more conside-ration. As for her, she came into focus for me; I mean, things progressed that night truly in the way they do in such situations, her scorpion tattoo the preface to her body.

All performances took place on this wide stage: a semicircle 5 metres in diameter, upholstered in red carpet, right in the middle of the large hall. The wall overlooking the stage was a mirror. I don't know what came over me at the end of the night. I made her stand up naked, and pressed her body against the mirror, with her back to me. In her small handbag, I found a lipstick and traced her hips. Tenderly I pulled her back to me, leaving behind an evident space between two red strokes outlining her curves with the utmost precision. After that she went to her room on one of the floors above the dance hall, and the next day (just as she said she would when she kissed me goodnight) she returned to her home, to Paris.

She disappeared into thin air. No address, nothing. And if it hadn't been for the lipstick lines on the mirror in the morning, I would have thought it all a dream.

During the day, my supervisor came round, saw the lines on the mirror and diplomatically gave in to his curiosity.

'You're an artist?' he asked.

'I'm trying.'

'With lipstick?' he continued, his curiosity now bare-faced mockery. We smiled, he for his reasons, me for mine, and with a tissue I wiped away the remnants of the night before.

After some time had passed, she began to reappear in my dreams. Often, she would come back, sleeping beside me as she did that night. As soon as I would start to touch her tattoo, it would slip through my fingers like a real scorpion, cobalt, small, sliding quickly along the curves of her backside. Hastily it would scurry along the red carpet, running, running towards the mirror until it would come to a halt at its bottom edge and begin to persistently attempt climbing towards the figure outlined in lipstick.

The scorpion would try, try a dozen times, as if it wanted to climb up to take its rightful place on the body as a tattoo— a real scorpion on the outline of a body! But the mirror's smooth surface continuously foiled its repeated stubborn attempts to do something seemingly impossible, nonsensical, crazy, foolish. I don't know what it was, but it was exhausting and painful, more like deadly.

While I watched on, the scorpion tried and tried with a peculiar stubbornness, scrambling upwards, only to slide back down until, overcome with fatigue, until it dripped sweat, it fell down, flung onto its back, moving his head and limbs with a desperate slowness, movements almost seemingly mechanical, as if they were its last . . . at that exact instant I wake up from my dream, my throat dry, drenched in sweat, sapped of energy.

Isn't this a novel-esque dream or a dream of a novel? I've asked myself so many times. Always, I've thought the answer is yes and often I have had the desire, to try and try again . . . only to hesitate and put it off, always for another day.

## THE SCORPION'S WRITINGS

That's it. I'll start. No genuine excuse for hesitation. I approached the window of the small metal shack at the private parking lot's entrance, next to the Al-Manara lion monument in downtown Ramallah. Mustering the best of my manners, I tried to disguise my hesitation, saying to the young man selling tickets, 'I'd like to sit over there, right between the two yellow lines drawn on the parking lot asphalt, that spot specifically.' I gestured to the very place. 'I want to sit there, and I'll pay you like any other driver, one dollar, meaning I want to park. I'm ready to sit on the ground, or at most I'll bring a plastic chair along.'

The parking attendant didn't attend to what I had said. Baffled, he soon assumed an aggressive demeanour; maybe as a defence mechanism to behaviour he found insulting. 'A respectable parking lot is what this is! How do you want to park when you don't even have a car and you're *not* a car?'

'Just think of me as a car,' I said, trying to lighten the mood to gain some time to win him over.

'Not until you've convinced me. What if someone thinks you're a spy, watching people? What would I tell my boss? What do I say to the customer if the parking lot says full and there's still an empty spot with someone sitting in it like that, out in the open?'

(The lot was actually uncovered, visible to the inner lively roads next to Al-Manara Square.)

'You wouldn't comprehend if I told you. What would you think if I told you that I'm trying to be a mirror, for example? What would you make of that?'

'What do I care if you want to be a mirror or a pile of mirrors, if I don't get why?'

The young man's offhand response caught me off guard and, after a pointless discussion, we agreed that he'd call his supervisor, the man who manages the lot, working nights, guarding it, sleeping in the small metal shack painted blood-red.

He came, round-shaped head, sturdy frame, his serious features rough—must be forty-something. I saw him and wasn't encouraged.

'What's the problem?' he posed the question directly at me.

'No problem. I want to rent out a spot like any car owner, but I want to sit there instead, to contemplate, just to have a think, and maybe write something, a novel maybe. I'll pay you.'

The man's features relaxed, his surliness melting into a gentle grin.

'You? A writer? Come, have some tea and let's talk it over. Come on. Me, I claim without much proof, that I'm a formidable reader! Do you know the meaning of formidable?' he asked his eyes fixed on mine like two nails in a plank of wood. (Nails and wood? What kind of simile is that?) 'A formidable reader, even though I'm a mule.' He shook with laughter. 'Come on, let's have a drink in the shack.'

'A formidable reader ... and a mule ... how?'

'Before, I was a determined mule of the revolution, but when that ended, I consciously and voluntarily remained a mule. Simple.'

(I shied away from getting into political, philosophical or historical discussions about the revolutions, their geneses or endings. As usual, I wasn't moved by any idealist assertion. My experience with masks is a long one, and I don't automatically side with the margin simply because it's the margin. Marginality for me isn't in itself valuable, and those who boast of it fail to gain my trust. Rather, my musings have revealed to me that the margin is no less cruel to the margin of the margin than the centre itself is to the margin.)

'No one else dares to call me a mule. You could say such a label is out of protest, or educational, or an outlet. I'll spell it out: I'm an old fighter, a liberated prisoner, freed in '95. I chose to live my own way, so I work as a guard, gateman and supervisor of this parking lot here instead of relying on any job benefit, which my past entitles me to. But what's your story? Why don't you write at home? Does inspiration only strike you here?' he asked jokingly.

'It seems as much. There are places in life that are for one's dreams only, you feel that they hold the keys to your imagination—such places drug you so you dream, summoning your dreams, enticing them. Or maybe, more precisely, such places allow you to dream these dreams. Compact places, magnetic, something like that. I had wanted one day to write next to or in a dance hall—the scorpion's birthplace—which captivated me, but it wasn't possible, and with time I raised this place or it raised me but . . .'

'Sure, I'll help you, and maybe you'll help me by giving me a rare chance to be present at the birth of a novel, or something like it. Ah yes . . . that's what I want. Eighteen years behind bars, reading, reading, but never managing to write anything, at least I should see something being written.'

'Deal.'

That's how I started coming here, and he in the evenings to settle with the parking lot attendant the day's 'fruit' before coming over to examine my 'fruit'. Each time he would find an excuse to inquire, ask for an explanation, suggest something or chat. At first, I'd manoeuvre myself so his voice wouldn't reach me so clearly, but later on I didn't find it necessary.

On the second day after my agreement with the 'freed prisoner', I resorted to trying to write about the scorpion, its empty spaces, its dances, dreams, travails, curses and other things that, to me, belonged to its world. It was then that I noticed something at once entertaining and strange: the parking lot owner came to know of our agreement and took a decision, which translated into a placard at the entrance facing the street, a huge cardboard sign, written on it in thick blue letters, PARK YOUR CARS AND PEOPLE HERE.

## 3

## PAINS BEFORE SCORPION'S BIRTH

I've never known, and maybe I never will, whether 'her womb' was the 'sad one'—according to female explanations for this barrenness—or if it was his testicles, or maybe something else altogether with no relation whatsoever to those two places, that made me my parents only child.

Apparently, it's because of him, my father I mean. He began his career as a construction labourer and swiftly became a mason. He started to get his ducks in a row to become an independent contractor who wouldn't answer to anyone but himself. A few months before leaving the company that he had worked for, he absentmindedly trod on a plank with a nail in it, which sunk deep into the sole of his foot. Yelling, the workers crowded him. Rather than taking him to a doctor, they treated him—as he requested—as they do on construction sites: they raised his foot and beat it with a wooden plank, using average force to expel the contaminated blood, and cauterized the wound with a cigarette stub.

It seemed like it was over, but it was just the beginning.

The wound grew infected and festered. Things quickly escalated and gangrene devoured his left leg in one fell swoop, all the way to just above his knee.

I was his first child and became his last. Afterwards, the 'mountain women' explained the sudden barrenness with 'her womb is sad'—my mother's womb—because of the dreadful event, especially as it happened not too long after my birth. They believed that, if a newly nursing mother tasted great grief, then her womb could end up distraught, its muscles shrivelling up, rejecting any new pregnancy.

Later on, I contemplated how they humanized the womb and personified it. In general, they would treat the womb as a separate being, not simply an organ. Maybe that's why they called it 'mother of children', even humanizing other things that came after birth: they'd call the milk gushing out of a mother's breasts 'milk wedding', for instance.

The result: my father lived with one leg while I lived as an orphan branch of our family tree. His leg 'flew off' with the strike of a nail. For years he had hammered nails into wood, so a nail hammered him, one nail, as if taking revenge on behalf of the world's nails.

I could politicize the matter by saying a landmine left behind by the occupying army blew off his leg, or that he was injured in combat with the same army in an intifada. But it isn't like that; there are naturally painful things that happen under occupation, just as without it, a leg can be cut off because of nails, or for other reasons.

Akin to how there's no symbolism in the conflict of generations, the fact that his leg was 'crippled' isn't a symbol of the political powerlessness of my father's generation, as opposed to mine, which is known for the 1987 Intifada. I don't ascribe at all to the political impotence of my father and his generation as it's presented sometimes for the necessities of that historical period; often I feel that what they accomplished according to their circumstances and the means they had is no less than what our generation managed.

It's a tale of an ordinary amputation of a real and ordinary leg of flesh and bone. The nail, which seems neutral in the eyes of the people it hasn't attacked, is the perpetrator and my actual adversary. So, since that day, I've despised nails, whether in wooden planks or brand new in tins, pounded into coffins or stuck in the walls of run-down houses to hang clothes, baskets, braids of garlic; or even Joha's infamous nail itself.

My mother wasn't defensive about her infertility, falling into a deep silence instead.

As if her motherhood ending with me wasn't enough, I had to be born on an unusual date, limiting my real birthday to once every four years. I was born on 29 February 1972. For my mother, my birthday was a myth. She celebrated it every year on 28 February, but each celebration was somewhat sombre. The ones she was most effusive about as a mother were the leap-year ones: the number 29 would roll round on diaries, newspaper pages and television screens—which she recorded of course with a different sort of flourish, in chalk at the top of the blackboard in the village girls' school where she taught.

It's a perfectly real date, an ordinary day in an ordinary year, with no symbolic dimension to it. I can rewind a bit to 1967, for example, for the cutting off of my father's leg to symbolize stolen land, etc. But no, it's 1972, the year of my birth, a neutral year, historically speaking, and it's my father's leg in particular that I've always wanted to talk about, a real leg knocked off by a nail. This leg itself, discarded and becoming a fistful of dirt, never really inhabited me; rather, what lives in me is the emptiness left behind by the amputated leg. Such horrible emptiness . . . how it weighs me down!

Because my father's leg had been amputated and as I found myself alone, two monstrous burdens fell on my small shoulders, which I was never able to completely shake off. The first was my biological mission, which I had always understood without anyone telling me outright; it seeped into my consciousness early on, from the men that visited my father and the ladies who frequented my mother and my aunt's company. From their stories and chats, I picked up on the mission of marriage and procreation to protect my 'father's tree'. 'The only branch on the tree,' the men would say. 'A lonely shoot,' the women would chorus. The way the women put it seemed more precise and intimate.

I ran away from this curse, but it didn't leave me be, because I was understanding of my father's desire, and my mother's especially. I couldn't conform to that role, and yet I couldn't condemn them. I consequently aborted the mission, without breaking away from the sadness.

I grew up with my father's cut-off leg, and it took me some time to grasp the meaning of its absence, which was familiar. But what brought me even closer to it was the other burden—painful, ugly and bizarre—that my father grew accustomed to laying on me unintentionally. Early on, I accepted the burden to attract love, praise and favours, but afterwards I kept on doing so without a choice, entangled, and sometimes out of pity. What it was was that my father got used to me scratching the sole of his foot, not his right foot that was still there but the foot of the cut-off leg. I don't mean the stump but the space across from the other present foot. 'Scratch the bottom of my cut-off leg, son, scratch it.' So I would scratch the bottom end of the emptiness until he was satisfied.

I would scratch the emptiness without differentiating between this part or that one, but my father would proffer precise directions to scratch specific parts of the emptiness, 'Go back a bit, down a few centimetres, up a bit . . .' as if he were directing me to precise points on a real sole. He'd also orchestrate how hard I was scratching and how quickly, as was needed!

In our family, scratching is a custom passed down from one generation to the next, like any other unexplained human habit: smoking, biting fingernails, cracking knuckles.

There are many passed-down habits in the village's families that are known to everyone. For example, if you walk next to a member of one of the families while he's explaining something to you, expect a rapid, painful jab in your shoulder. Spontaneously, his hand will stretch towards your shoulder—whenever things get heated, or he wants to emphasize something or deny something—to firmly poke you with the index finger of his taut hand.

Scratching is our family's lot, an essential and deep-rooted custom, so much so that no one recalls this masculine demand as exceptional, and even how it's done is known to the villagers: the elder man lies down (the grandfather or father) and asks the young ones to scratch the bottom of his feet most of the time or—at latter stages of his life, when things have deteriorated—his back. But as for someone asking you to scratch the foot of their cut-off leg, that's something inconceivable.

The bother of scratching, which bequeathed me a particular relationship with that at-once-present-and-absent leg as well as an individual penchant for emptiness, was the other burden I tried to run away from. As for the bother of preserving the family line, meaning getting married and having kids, the more I felt them imposing on me, the more I entertained death; the more they wanted me to be an extension of them (in not so many words), the more I wanted to be myself. That's why my secondary-school studies were turbulent; I completed them with difficulty and, at a very early age, I began to seek refuge in the mountain.

My father almost never spoke of his cut-off leg that had been devoured by maggots. Rather, it happened that he mentioned a few times the protrusions on his stump, criticizing the doctor, doubting his competency, recalling other amputees he saw when getting his prosthetic leg fitted, and how tremendously precise their amputations had been. His descriptions of the 'aesthetics' of others' amputations dripped with barely veiled envy.

*

'Isn't it enough that you've cut off his leg? Now you want to cut off his family line, too?' the 'prisoner' asked me, affronted.

'Whose leg? Whose line?'

'Your father's leg and his line, or maybe your character's, I don't know.'

I was at a loss. Why didn't 'the prisoner' engage with what I had written as a description of memories, instead of considering it an aggressive act or a literary aggression? Rather than growing angry or expelling him from the outline of the novel, on the contrary, his violent outburst endeared him to me, making me aware of his sensitive disposition and his audacity. 'You weren't able to stomach a few lines about him,' I continued, 'but I'm the one who scratched that emptiness for years . . . I don't blame you. It's something that takes a bit of patience to come into focus. This is my life, my story: it has a lot of drama, successive doses of profound distress, and a lot of peculiarity, to the extent that I continually imagine myself a mere character in the novel, choreographed by the hand of a brilliant writer, but he overburdens me with unusual loads. I don't mean in a literary sense—that's for the critics—I'm talking on a human and personal level. He always puts me in the most complex scenarios, boiling over with seemingly cosmic plots, or at least in pivotal points of tearful collective historical plots, always overturning places on my head. If I were the narrator, I would distribute the load among many protagonists. I understand your solidarity with my father, because in the end it's a way of showing solidarity with me.

'A nail. A short-lived, filthy, used, rusted, twisted, "brother of a whore" nail in rotten, crummy, mangled wood in a crummy near-finished construction site is behind this whole disaster, that's what cut off his leg and his line, not me.'

'Sorry, I didn't mean to put you out or pull you down. I was just expressing my pain, but you piqued my curiosity: had your father lost a bit of his mind to ask you to scratch a foot that was no longer there? Shouldn't his being a father to an only child have prevented him from drowning you in this strange ritual?'

'It has nothing to do with lunacy, or conspiracy. He probably didn't expect it would leave such an impression on me. Who among us knows what traces our acts leave on others? In life, prologues never have the same outcomes because it's impossible that these prologues are ever exactly identical!'

My father was missing his leg, I grew up with that and he got used to it. But we, as I said, are a family where the tradition of rubbing, massaging and scratching is entrenched. It awakens at middle age, or at my age, and begins to slowly grow worse until it reaches an irritating stage. But as soon as one of us grows up in normal conditions, he finds himself drowned by grandchildren. With a little bit of cunning and luring, grandparents are able to put the little ones to task and at the same time pass down the tradition. I was both the children and the grandchildren.

This 'penchant' wasn't particularly pronounced for my father, but rather suppressed to a great extent it seemed—limited to the bottom of the emptiness of his leg; generally, he wasn't insistent on the matter—he'd ask for it once or twice a week, for several minutes. But one day I discovered by chance that his unfulfilled need to be scratched might explode all at once.

That day, it happened that his yearning to be scratched had overtaken him in my absence. My mother was visiting the village and I had gone up to the top of the mountain to take part in shepherding sheep with other children my age and to contemplate the view. The view was absolutely breathtaking from that ridge open to the horizons, the end of which was the sea to the west, and from the east, mountains came clearly into view, which I had often heard were the Al-Salt range in Jordan.

Once back, I came across him seated, trying to scratch the emptiness with the toes of his right foot. He was exhausted to the point that I was scared of approaching and intervening, so I stood and observed him from afar: he tried and tried a dozen times; he kept on trying and trying with a peculiar stubbornness until, overcome with fatigue, until he dripped sweat, he fell down, flung onto his back, moving his head and limbs with a desperate slowness, movements almost seemingly mechanical, as if they were his last.

He terribly needed it, it seemed. But I couldn't tie my entire fate to scratching the bottom of a non-existent foot, despite the very real space it occupied for him. Similar to how my lengthy meditations on the nature of this ritual, and my inability to understand it, frustrated me: the family ritual of scratching on the one hand and my father's more advanced version (scratching the emptiness) on the other.

Everything to do with my father happened quite normally when taking into consideration the size of his handicap. He was extremely sensitive to anyone or anything passing through the space left behind by his amputated leg; it would drive him mad. We got used to paying attention to it, as if the leg were still there. With the onset of the handicap, my father adopted a curious measure: he left the centre of the village for the mountain, rather than staying in a flat area, which would have suited him more. One day, he said he couldn't stand the roads any more. Abandoning the small apartment he had at the heart of our extended family, he built us a house on the highest reaches of the village mountain (actually the highest mountain in the centre of Palestine), a house which, in addition to the levelling out of the rugged path to it, consumed all the injury compensation from the construction company along with nearly all of his savings.

Up there, we owned a large plot of land, in the middle of which was an enormous cave, the talk of many a story and legend. People would compare it to an old man's laughing mouth, but to me it was more like a lion's yawn. In any case they called it 'Mountain Gob'. It's right by there that my father, without his leg, built our house. Maybe he wanted to distance himself and his misfortune from people, but they came to him. Next to the house he fashioned a small pen where he raised livestock, getting help from a shepherd. With time, he learnt how to adjust places to his handicap, and started to take part in producing cheeses, milk products, among other things.

My mother was a science teacher at the village girls' school, not having much time to do much with him. We all did what we could. A very good standard of living. But a child like me could see the tears pooling in his mother's eyes as she held my hand and took me down the mountain every morning to school.

Had her womb grown forlorn or had his testicles?

When my father grew older, and diabetes took his sight (the 'prisoner' interrupted me, half-joking, half-commiserating this time, 'Now you want to extinguish the light of his eyes?'), he developed an odd habit: whenever he had a visitor, he'd cover his body and face in a blanket (grass green) completely. Only his hands would move around outside it and gesture while he spoke. It's possible what saved them from also being veiled, unfortunately, was my father's vice of smoking. He would smoke under the blanket, suffocating himself, whenever someone visited us. My father didn't allow anyone other than me, my mother and my aunt, to see anything of him, except his hands, after he lost his sight. And when he was asked about why he covered himself, he'd simply reply, 'I can no longer see you, so why do you need to see me?'

## 4

## THIRD DANCE OF THE SCORPION

One evening, I went to my remarkable 'office' amid cars looking nothing alike, whose drivers' looks varied along with their reactions as they saw me seated there in my curious fashion. The 'prisoner' was out in front of his shack, kindling fire in a metal bin. I asked him for permission to enter and took my plastic chair. I put it carefully in the middle of the empty parking space between the two yellow lines, in the exact same place as usual.

He must have noticed the extreme care with which I placed my chair. 'I was going to leave you to your own thing,' he said. 'Or at least stifle my curiosity, but I noticed that you're not satisfied with just placing your chair anywhere between the two yellow lines. Instead, you place it in a precise square between the lines that never shifts, as if it's sacred. So what's the deal with your golden square?'

'Yes, there's a story there. I was planning on writing it, but I'll tell it to you. Come have a seat.'

With a fire alight in his bin, he came over. We sat there, chatting and warming ourselves up while he fed the fire with bits of smashed wooden crates that he'd usually collect from the nearby vegetable stall.

'About four years ago, when part of this lot was an old two-storey building, very small really, its ground floor had a separate entrance: consisting of two rooms, a kitchen and a bathroom. There were ten suspended steps, starting from a landing in line with the pavement, leading to another floor of the same area (some 70 square meters): a small abode with a bedroom, a sitting room (with several mismatched sofas and a wooden bench wide enough to seat three), a kitchen I never entered, and a bathroom indicated by a small pencil sketch of a naked man with his back turned at such an angle, you could see the stream of urine gushing out arc-like. That was the only drawing hung up in that abode.

'The building belonged to a man I'm sure you know better than me, the investor and owner of this parking lot. This plot of land, as everyone knows, is now located on the most expensive kilometre in Palestine, maybe even the most expensive in the Middle East. What irked your friend is that the building had been rented out for many years at a symbolic price to a man from the villages of the North, a man in love with that abode.

'After the Oslo Accords, when the Palestinian Authority was established with its administrative apparatus and Ramallah entered the "machine" of the new world economy, the rent for an apartment in this place went up tenfold. But what pained your friend even more is that, without exaggeration, the price for the land itself was valued in the millions. According to my sources, he offered a quarter of a million dollars to the tenant to move out, but he refused.

'The tenant loved this building on the one hand, and on the other, the millions didn't interest him. Quite simply, he didn't want the money. He would live on the bottom floor, and sometimes on the upper one, but most of the time, for many years, he rented out the top floor to people passing through. Rumours spread that I can't confirm (maybe in an attempt to explain why he refused the quarter million dollars) that he would host foreign young women; those who came to Birzeit University on student exchanges, or to learn Arabic, employees of international organizations, journalists or others. It's said that on the ground floor he kept a large world map, where many of the countries—most even—were marked with an 'X', because every time things were 'successful' with a young foreign woman, he crossed off the country she came from. He wasn't far off from having 'slept' with women of every nationality.

'It's still all just hearsay! But what I do know and what interests me is that a great writer during the years that I lived in Ramallah rented the upper room every year for long periods so he could write. We would go to him: young students at Birzeit University—men and women—budding writers; intellectuals in the making; lost ones searching for answers to strange questions; simpletons searching for questions to ask; curious people; those residing in the city and those returning from exile; well-off folk searching for meaning in things that they themselves didn't know; salesmen, yes, salesmen, of everything that comes to mind.

'As for the tenant, the "playboy", he rarely came to such get-togethers, barely opening his mouth. He would listen, attentively it appeared, not listening in a foolish or condescending manner, nor fascinated. Apart from the "sexual internationalism" that was attributed to him, his attachment to the place and his refusal of the quarter million dollars, he didn't say or do anything worth mentioning. He had refused the quarter million dollars despite his financial situation that was by no means exceptional in that era. Yes, he had a reasonable salary for many years as an employee at a middle-grade administrative post in an international organization, but it was the new Ramallah, the centre of the new administrative apparatus and the private sector, with all its posts that we didn't know before. A downpour of money from which bloomed a spring of construction in the form of high towers, luxury villas and institutional buildings, but the stubbornness of this man prevented your friend from harvesting the slightest piece of fruit from this spring.

'The 'great writer' was a school on two legs, open to all, improvised, portable and utterly free. We would go to him, he'd speak and we'd listen, we'd speak and he'd listen. In such sessions I learnt so much.'

'You mean Hussein Al-Barghouti?'

'Names aren't important, I wish you wouldn't ask me about names.'

'But Hussein's room, as far as I know, wasn't torn down; one could get to it by going down, down some not-hanging stairs. Why did you make the stairs hanging?'

(Silence.)

'Okay . . . Hussein (if you knew him), is it true that he was the master of a Sufi brotherhood?'

'No, he was the master of his own path.'

I go back to my topic. The 'great writer' fell ill and abandoned the room, only to die a few months later. Me, his friends, his disciples, and his followers never went back there. Whenever I passed by the abode on this road while shopping or out for a walk, I'd remember him. I'd always planned to ask the 'playboy' to rent me the spot so I could write there; I felt that it had the capacity to woo my dreams, my imagination, my memories.

A few days before the invasion of April 2002, I left for the mountain, and snuck back in a day before the partial lifting of the lengthy, ironclad lockdown that lasted three weeks. That day, I passed through here, shocked to find the hanging stairs leading to the room, destroyed. I don't know how they were destroyed or if they collapsed, eight steps (out of the original ten) no longer there. Only the step linked to the landing adjoined to the pavement and the step right by the threshold of the bedroom door remained. Iron rods and small lumps of concrete dangled chaotically from the two steps and between them an emptiness, a terrible emptiness that made my head spin whenever I stared at it, as if in a drunken haze. For me it was a heavy blow, but a godsend for your friend. The place where I wanted to write my novel had been mutilated.

I remember that day: I had snuck back into Ramallah; it was one of my seasonal and sudden games with death. I would change paths, guided by the rumble of the tanks—the soldiers wouldn't dare move around by any other means. Black asphalt roads were scarred with white tank tread marks. Devastation. All the cars on each roadside had been crushed by the tanks.

I saw this scene pristine, before the lifting of the lock-down or anything else could disturb it. Just like when people go out for the first time after snowfall: things are still virginal, the snow perfectly white, no footprints. The sight of the crushed cars was painful, but it was also somewhat striking.

Everything that was intact and new, you saw at once razed to the ground, reverted to its origins, reduced to heaps of iron. The cars that I was familiar with, that had been ordinary and uncontested in their form and presence in my memory for dozens of years, were no longer recognizable.

Such a scene is only possible in a cataclysmic context, a striking catastrophe.

Cars and vehicles of all makes, all models, all colours, belonging to a range of social classes, used for different purposes, some of them freshly imported with their nylon covers still on: all were one and the same after being spit out by the jaws of the tanks and army bulldozers. The cars were dreams, years of toil. So many dreams crushed that day on the pavement, dreams of iron and eight steps of emptiness.

Maybe the bulldozer driver had been fascinated by the sight of the hanging steps, then took aim and knocked it down with one or two blows during the smashing of cars and dreams. Maybe. No one saw it. Maybe. It's just a possibility out of a million others. (I like to verify things before holding the occupier responsible for anything.)

You and I are now sitting exactly where the steps fell. Its emptiness still leads to the abode 'of dreams' without leading to it. But I didn't anticipate what happened next. . . .

The 'playboy' couldn't conceive that the stairs could be restored, or replaced, or that reaching the upper floor was possible with an iron ladder, for example. He would tell mutual friends (whom I've never met) that if any other stairs were put in, they wouldn't be the same ones that he had always climbed up on. In some cases, he didn't even want to admit that the stairs were gone. Quite often he would try, especially at the end of the night, to go up to the room: he would set foot on the landing adjoining to this street here, climb onto the first step that hadn't collapsed, and continue climbing, stepping into the emptiness which would only betray him, and would tumble to the ground. He would then go back to the landing, then the first step, to stumble again in the emptiness. He tried and tried a dozen times, he kept on trying and trying with a peculiar stubbornness until overcome with fatigue, until he was dripping with sweat, and fell down, flung onto his back, moving his head and limbs with a desperate slowness, movements almost seemingly mechanical, as if they were his last.

He didn't see the emptiness, or he didn't want to see it, so he kept on stepping and stepping, and stumbling and stumbling. Perhaps the loss of the steps terrified him; I know perfectly well and better than any other person what he felt—I know all too well the weight of emptiness.

For me as well, it wasn't a trivial matter as, for so long, I had wanted to rent out this abode when my faltering financial circumstances would allow it, that is, to write there as the 'great author' had. That's after the dance hall (scorpion's birthplace) was no longer an option.

The destruction of the stairs saddened me, its emptiness pulling me to the place even more, but as for the tenant, he was utterly shattered. His family came, I was told, and took him back with them; I don't know how they managed to convince him to return to his village in the North. All I do know is that he refused to accept even a penny for vacating the place.

You can even ask your boss. An opportunity like this, he hadn't even dared to dream of in his wildest dreams. Without hesitation he razed the entire dwelling to the ground and transformed it temporarily into a parking lot. Nothing was left. No trace of the place it once was, no witnesses. It was a complete place to begin with, then the stairs were lost and after that everything disappeared. I came here, to the place of the stairs, to its emptiness, specifically to write my novel, a novel about a scorpion chasing an empty space between two lines on a mirror, about an emptiness I scratch for my father. Here, I came across an emptiness that a man in full possession of his mental faculties tripped over, and I've arrived at a black empty spot between two yellow lines, would you look at that!

## 5

# AT THE SCORPION'S BIRTHPLACE
# IS WHERE IT HAPPENED

Most certainly, he wasn't able to enter the celebration hall or the dance hall (as I like to call it) unless disguised, and through the main wide door or through the entrance reserved for those invited. I know the entrances well: the first, an entrance from the right-hand side closed with a screen door. I was among those who had the right to use its key to set merchandise down in the kitchen and return the key.

The second entrance was the main one, in the middle. The third one was on the left, an elegant glass door, exclusively reserved for the guests of the celebration hall. It only opened at night and I wasn't allowed to use its key.

I was in the village the day the young man infiltrated the hall. I remember that I had left Ramallah for a few days, following medical advice, to rest my nerves from my daily relationship with the news of death and death itself. At that time, hysterical anxiety attacks afflicted me nightly, and my body started to show signs of skin diseases usually linked to psychological stress (eczema and a type of ringworm). You could say that I was tired of death.

I worked in those days as an editor of a news website, as the only subordinate of an intrepid editor-in-chief who tired me out but was thrilling all the same. Back from America with a reasonable amount of money, he invested in a project that, from the beginning, I doubted had any commercial prospects. As for him, he had always dreamt of working in media and believed that his moment had arrived.

I wasn't convinced of the quality of the project, but in the end he gave me a reasonable salary. It wasn't easy for me to find this type of work, what with the seasonal recklessness that threw my secondary-school studies into disarray, and put an end to my university degree, depriving me of my diploma, even though all I needed was one more term.

When it came to work, my time was unrestricted. I would sleep in the office, in an isolated state I grew addicted to. In some sense, I also felt that I had a role, in the nationalistic sense of the word, even if on the margins of this 'war' (taking a bit of liberty with the word) after having been right in the thick of the previous Intifada. I used to be in the news, and now I just report it, just cover it.

I would leave the office when events outside heated up, to touch them, to smell them, including the burnt bodies in cars bombed from above. I would write articles and news reports under pen names.

The website ran decently well up to a point, but the gamble taken by the editor-in-chief was more than was reasonable. During its period of establishment (in the mid-90s), there was a boom in the Internet and tech worlds. The man believed that a historical revolution in media had arrived, and was one of the first to take the initiative with this type of medium, but the winds don't always blow the way the ship wants. The site had many visitors but advertising practices weren't developed to the extent of making news websites commercially successful.

Despite everything, the editor-in-chief continued to pay my salary and to rent the office, only to wake up one day two years later from his media dream on the verge of bankruptcy.

It was (the day when the young man infiltrated the hall) one of my sad days in the village. I cried so much that day, maybe because I was seeing the place for the first time since my aunt's death—the situation at hand and dangers on the road had prevented me from attending her burial a few months prior. Maybe I cried because I felt that the end of my father and mother was approaching, or that I'd grown older than I should have. My father was gaunt, my mother too—something had been extinguished in them. I looked differently at the leg of emptiness, an emptiness filled by a prosthetic leg. The leg was inside the house, while my father was outside, sunning himself in front of the cave. I remember asking him, 'Where's your other leg, Baba?'

'It fell ill, son. The doctor removed it, cut if off.'

'What an animal.'

'No, no, sickness is the animal, my son, if he hadn't cut it off I'd be dead.'

'Why didn't he implant another one in its place?'

My father just laughed.

Remembering that, I embraced the prosthetic leg with great affection, playing with its leather straps as I used to when I was young. In silence I cried bitterly. The leg seemed smaller than usual, much smaller than what was engraved in my memory.

In my childhood, they warned me against touching it while it was parked in a corner or up against a wall so it wouldn't fall on me. I remember a time when it towered over me, terrifying. The more I grew, the smaller it became until I started carrying it, bringing it closer to my father or pushing it out of the way for my mother. Often, my father would say, aggravated or mischievously, 'Bring me the fractured one, the ripped out one, the cut-off one.' And now I embrace it, looking at it from above, lightweight in my hands, a leg embodying that void once filled with a real leg. It really was a statue, a literal statue of my father's amputated leg, filling the void whose bottom I had scratched for so long.

I cried, the paradox distressing me: a complete body, whose leg was cut off and buried before its time, and then this artificial leg, evidence of the emptiness. Some day, the body of my father would die completely, turning into a pile of soil and only this leg would remain as a witness to his past.

I imagined his death; if he died before me, would I bury his leg with him or keep it as an incomplete statue of an incomplete body, or fix it to a stone plinth on the mountain in front of our cave, making it into a complete statue of my father's body?

I saw graves as stone metaphors, sculptures, a final attempt to delay the eternal absence, like a memory in stone of the absolute emptiness left behind by the disappearance of the body. I visited my grandfather's grave for the first time in a long while. The stones that I had remembered as white and radiant were now tarnished, nearly black. The date of his death inscribed on the grave terrified me: 1 December 1979.

How well I remember that day. I had just started school, my first days there, when my grandfather visited me on the mountain. He was eager to see my clothes for my Year-One class. He turned each piece over one by one and kissed them before letting me know how happy he was and congratulating me. He went back down the mountain and died a few weeks later.

I remember his funeral in great detail: how he was washed, prayed over, a crowd taking part (by village standards). I remember the sound of feet, dozens of them, maybe hundreds of feet of those carrying the bier, and those walking behind him, striking the earth and kicking up a suffocating cloud of dust. The friction of the shoes of those paying their last respects against the ground created different sounds that dissipated the austere silence. Each sound unique based on the type of sole, the weight of the wearer and where they trod: on the asphalt or the dirt pavement. Many feet that kept plodding along regardless of the gap of a single foot, that of my father's. Hundreds of feet, most of them men of our family, feet addicted to the peculiar masculine habit of scratching.

I remember from that funeral, after the burial, a woman recounting a bad omen. She said that she had seen the coffin shouldered by the men (the women walked behind) pitching and swaying, tottering, meaning that there would soon be another death in the village. Many long years passed until I was freed from the link between a teetering coffin and the imminent death of others. Other people will always die in the village, it dawned on me with some irritation.

After that solemn visit to my grandfather's grave that afternoon, I went to the centre of the village. Leaning against the electric pylon in the middle of the main roundabout that had become the village's commercial hub, I remembered many things. Scenes flashed past in my memory, night scenes of which I was a part: before dawn I was standing there, waiting, like hundreds of others, for a workers' bus or a shared taxi to shuttle us to cities on the Mediterranean coast, nameless on old maps (or to the 'West' the workers would say playfully) or 'Scorpion Land', my scorpion, as I had come to call it.

Drawling voices, people coming from afar that you could make out from the gleaming stubs of their cigarettes (like the one that had cauterized my father's foot), embers lighting up the darkness of a village whose sole transformer wasn't enough to light up the streets. The sole lamp affixed to the central pylon illumined the surly workers' faces. Some faces were optimistic while others contended against laziness and life's hardships with coarse jokes. 'May God screw up this day,' one youth quipped. Another suggested hefting the pylon onto his back and carrying on. One labourer asked another to stretch out his vocal cords so he could hang his wet underwear on them; a young man threw out a surrealist phrase, 'Don't look at me with that loud tone!' Another, in the attempt to describe the tragedy of the scene, philosophized,

'Now I know why Ibn Khaldoun wrote such a long Muqad-dimah before actually starting his book: of course he wanted to describe a scene like this.'

I remember my very early departure to the labour market. The scratching perturbed me and I wanted to break away from the excessive worry over me, so I set out to search for a life of my own. I went to where people set off from, walking through the only cramped lane left open by the occupier for those who wanted work.

New shops in the heart of the village, Atari games, the beginnings of a cafe. But the people were dull, their clothes dull, because of the general situation, consecutive sieges and atrocious unemployment. I took in the collective landscape, duller than usual, and in the children's eyes I made out signs of malnourishment, their complexions yellowing, skin rife with disease.

The owner of the barbershop explained to me (maybe because I was a sort of journalist) that the onset of poverty could be detected in the change of hair-cutting habits. So whoever cut his hair once or twice a month made it last for longer, and whoever used to get his hair and beard cut in the barbershop grew content with getting only a haircut.

The place itself had changed a lot: massive pine trees that had hosted generations of villagers beneath its branches were ripped out to make way for bigger roads; many farming roads built by the 'agricultural relief committees' now joining up the hills and mountains until the construction sprawl reached our home, which for many long years seemed like a monastery suspended between the earth and the sky.

On my left was a newly built prestigious girls' secondary school that, as indicated by the enormous metal plaque, had been funded by a European institution and Japanese donors. On my right, a large new mosque built entirely from donations from the local community. I folded in with people in the cafe and out in front of the shops to the extent that my social skills and mood permitted me.

That evening, on my way to the house (going up the mountain on foot tired me out even though the road seemed shorter than what it was when I was a child or even an adolescent, even the mountain itself seemed smaller), I received a text sharing breaking news. Whoever sent the message didn't know that the news affected me personally. I raced to reach the top of the mountain and went immediately to the television, wanting to know as soon as possible where it happened exactly. It was the third time that I've had such an experience this year, the coincidence landing me anew in a hellish pit of inextricable plots. The only probability to impact me directly occurred, instead of a million other possibilities: a disguised youth infiltrated the celebration hall, the dance hall, the hall of my scorpion, the scorpion that sweated. With the click of a button, he killed himself, thirty other lives and the place, too.

## 6

## COMMENTARY ON THE
## SCORPION'S 'TRAGEDY'

The 'prisoner' said to me in a somewhat reproachful tone, 'Why lie? If you're talking about real-life things, why don't you just call them as they are? In the beginning, you talked about a dance hall, which in reality is a celebration hall, and you said it's in a building, but whoever follows the news in this country knows it's a hotel. Aren't you actually talking about the attack on the Netanya Hotel, which was basically the pretext for the April 2002 invasion?'

'Names aren't that important, believe me, usually there are no names in my novel, haven't you noticed that? Names are constraints for the characters and me, I don't like them. I prefer to describe my characters according to what sets them apart. Then, my friend, you want a novelist to write "real-life things". Listen: in order to be able to speak the truth, you have to wait for a lot of people to die; in the same way, speaking the truth may end up killing a lot of people.

'Narration is dangerous, very dangerous indeed—there are usually masks and displacements involved, lies I mean.

'Narration is a matter of plots. Transforming the hall into a dance hall, the hotel into a building, are small tricks, part of fortifying the plot. In general, I'm fascinated by plots (not in their classical form, of course) because as I told you, I always feel like the victim, I see myself as a novelist's creation dropped into a series of extremely complicated and painful plots. I feel that in my life these plots are like ropes from the gallows wrapped around my neck. At the pinnacle of the plot, the execution takes place, but the cord is cut seconds before I suffocate. How else can you explain the date of my birthday, my father's leg being cut off, my loneliness, my relationship with emptiness, and how emptiness pursues me in this place that I loved that ended up being destroyed, and to top it off the explosion of "my hall"? A hundred-year-old conflict that insisted on exploding in those few personal square metres of mine! I wished that the war at least wouldn't come near that personal perimeter, but that's exactly what happened.

'Authors' ruses are like ambushes: you have to cover the bomb, camouflage it well and lie in wait for the moving target. The moment the target reaches the bomb, or a few moments before, you detonate it. When it comes to suicide vests, one's got to reconcile several things: keeping your cool until the final moment, the target's arrival, choosing the most crowded spot. There is no successful plot without precise camouflage and meticulous timing.

'Narration is dangerous, dangerous and frightening. Sometimes the plot has a murderer. I'm going to tell you a story that deeply affected me and taught me a lot. A true, forgotten story, which is basically the story of the village, or most of those who live there, a story that's not mentioned and which only a few of the elderly know, aside from me. Maybe because I'm a good listener or because those who love stories tend to search for collective memories and for the old in their private lives, as if they were collecting antiques or old trinkets. They often have the chance to come across precious and rare things.

'This must have been (I'm thinking) sometime between 1800 and 1850. Our great-grandfather and his many children lived in one of the villages of the south, the south of Palestine. He was a prominent and powerful notable, among the lords of the south, tyrannical too. His diwan served as a court where people were brought to trial, and at the diwan's entrance was a gallows built from large stones cut in the shape of a massive portico, which witnessed many hangings. Not too long ago, I heard that the portico still stands there in that village as a site of archaeological interest.

'Our polygamist great-grandfather sired many sons and daughters, one of the secrets of his power. It so happened that one of the daughters closest to his heart fell in love with a young man, but he refused to give him her hand in marriage. I don't know why, at least the story doesn't specify why, or maybe it just masked some of the details.

'After the girl fell into despair, she did something very unusual that, to those who understood the customs of the age, bordered on pure madness: she ran away from her father and sought refuge with the lord of a prominent rival family (smaller than our family and less influential) who had no choice but to grant her refuge. Because, as you know, in both Bedouin and pastoral tradition, to turn out a "guest" brings eternal opprobrium.

'At first, my great-grandfather tried to get his daughter back diplomatically, but it was no use, so the family resorted to other tactics. They sent my great-grandmother to that sheikh's house and, by some ruse, she tricked the sheikh's wife and was able to get her daughter to come outside, outside the house under a carob tree where two of her brothers lying in wait slit her throat and hacked her corpse to pieces.

'The sheikh wasn't at home. His wife quickly understood what had happened when she stepped out to have a look and found the body in pieces. What caught my attention was how the shrewd wife informed her husband of his guest's murder.

'The wife kept her wits about her despite the gravity of the situation, despite the chopped-up cadaver scattered in the courtyard. It is said that she prepared his favourite dish: mansaf with buttermilk rice. She received him calmly, removed his cloak and washed his feet, telling him that she had prepared something he liked, especially for him. In a corner just big enough for the two of them, she sat him down and took a seat facing him. As soon as he stretched out his hand to take his first bite, she flung a handful of black ash on the food, the exact place where his hand had been. With a start, he yanked his hand back and asked, "What is it?"

"Evil will follow you and your descendants till the Judgment Day, for your guest has been murdered."

He jumped up, cut a piece out of the woollen tent and put a hole through it. He then put his horse's neck through the hole, in accordance with the old Arab custom of asking for help. He roamed from one family to the next, "throwing the shame from his face to theirs" (as they used to say back then) and so many families assembled. After a bloody battle, my great-grandfather and his children were driven out from the south to the centre of the country. Arriving at the mountain, the mountain of my childhood, they joined the small village there. They grew up in that village and it grew larger with them.

'The way in which this woman told her husband the news was decisive to all that followed. Perhaps if she had told him in an ordinary manner, she would have given him time to think and hesitate, to weigh up the powers at play and the price to be paid. Perhaps his fury would have found an outlet here or there, maybe even holding her responsible. But she stuck him in a corner with no place to go, and at the moment he was about to have his first bite of a dish he loved, ravenous, she ruined his food in a theatrical fashion, almost ceremonial if one could call it that, as if she were telling him that he did not deserve to eat. The plot had closed in on him at the last moment, and smothered him.

'If not for this brilliant mise en scène of the girl's murder, I may not have been among the mountain dwellers at the centre of the country and things would be completely different.'

## (7)

## THE SCORPION'S ERASURE

Now, when I rub the scorpion tattoo in my dreams, it dissolves into black ash and sand, crunching under my fingertips. Painful sand. For some time, I've been worried about my scorpion, and I know now that my fear was justified. I had wished that the scorpion would escape from the curses of this war; with the anxiety of a mother over an only child (how well I know this anxiety), I implored the fates to allow me to raise him. In other words: I had wanted to complete my (aesthetic) project that had slipped off from a tattoo on the back of my first young woman, towards endings that I didn't know at all. I had wanted the scorpion to guide me to them, and wanted them to be aesthetic endings.

How can I still dream of the place, knowing that writing is a dream? Things were blown up and much blood was shed and, as my aunt the 'dream lady' of the mountain would say, 'If there's blood in a dream, then it's a rotten one.' There had been a pool of blood in my dream. My personal memory had exploded, the hall had shattered to pieces and the red carpet where I had slept for so long had been burnt, the red carpet that I had cleaned countless times on my knees with a small wet cloth in hand. The red carpet, from which the small cobalt scorpion had advanced towards the mirror smashed to bits, had burnt.

Human limbs were scattered, mixed up with the limbs of the young perpetrator, the stench of burnt flesh and gunpowder flooded the scorpion's nostrils and mine too. I know that smell very well from having covered the assassination of two young men of the Intifada burnt alive in their cars—I have often smelt it.

My father's leg was amputated, all alone, when the rusty nail struck it; in the hall bodies broke apart like a masbaha whose prayer beads skipped across the tables, under the chairs, and onto the marble floor, coming to a standstill in every place, even the platform where once upon time a carnal, feverish melody had been played.

Blood on the plates and glasses, on the tables that for more than a year I had prepared for celebrations, plates with blue borders reserved for meals with meat and plates with brown borders reserved for dairy products.

The stairs to the room in Ramallah were mutilated, fallen or made to fall—I don't know—leaving behind a tremendous emptiness, while the hall itself had been killed. Ever since I heard about the attack, I knew the place was dead, a place that had been for me . . . I mean my memory.

Would the scorpion be able to evacuate all those bodies?

Without knowing it, the young man stormed into the course of my story, got to 'my place' before me, killed himself, killed thirty people and killed a chapter of my story.

'Does that place mean *that* much to you? You might as well be delivering an elegy! Don't you know the rubble on which it's been built?' the prisoner asked me, a deep scarlet rippling across his cheeks.

'I tried to make those few square metres neutral. I tried to strip it of its collective history, for the sake of my own memory, my own time, my happy days. I tried to defend my right to love my memory, my right not to hate myself, not like Palestinian labourers who build for the one who destroys them, but rather as a person who loved the mirror where he traced the hips of his first woman, who loved the sea at the moment of sunset, the sand and seashells, the night breezes playing with the blue curtains of a hall where he had slept for more than a year.

'I protest against this plot, its bloody explosion in my private space, more bloody than I had ever imagined in any of my nightmares, more cruel than anyone could endure, actually more bloody and cruel than all the other plots that the narrator's hand had put me at the heart of.

'The explosion put me to the test, tested me in a way I'd been running away from for a long time. I had wanted to isolate this place from its environment, I had wanted to extract it from the frame of others' memories. I had wanted to celebrate my personal time there, or to understand it and immerse myself in it, to tell my story in this place in my own way, my schizophrenic relationship with it: I love it tremendously and return back to it in my dream, (the dream of the scorpion) more than you can imagine, and at the same time I hate its political context, I hate its collective framework, I hate the time others have spent here.

'Sometimes I think that I'm suffering from some form of schizophrenia or other, but it became clear that the place itself was schizophrenic, and it was just my sensitivity that was receptive to this psychosis. Or even if the place accosted me and attacked me with its schizophrenia more than others, and crushed me because of this curse of plots out to get me, I tried to dodge this misery, but the explosion reduced my margin, so much so it felt like nothing.

'My friend, someone who can love a place simply because he worked there as a dishwasher really feels for those who have been chased out of their homes, and understands what it means to have someone else sleeping in your warm bed, eating with your spoons and on your plates, drying their faces in your towel, desecrating their offspring's childhood with your children's stolen toys—all this I know. I wasn't neutral, especially in those days, when I worked in the hall, but that doesn't mean I won't talk about a personal experience, a curse that is my own, a rolling curse gaining momentum, of a particular kind, a particular taste.

'If you were searching for the occupation, it's in the background, and I can bring it to the foreground in everything, everything. I try to catch my breath a bit away from the occupation. When it comes to my father, I condemned the nail even though I could have easily politicized the matter. If I'd wanted I could have mentioned from the start that my father was forbidden from travelling to complete his studies at Beirut University, after having already completed two years. He left it all behind when they tried to blackmail him: he could only go back on the condition that he spy on our young male relatives living in Jordan and Lebanon.

'Mad about literature and philosophy, he had wanted to go far, so they assassinated his dream. He chose to spend his life as a labourer at Solel Boneh, in silence, to stay here, rather than sell his soul to the devil.

'Where possible, I tried to catch my breath a bit away from this contaminated air but, you see, here I am suffocated by the smell of burnt flesh mixed with gunpowder that even followed me to my scorpion's home. In a war like this, even places lose their neutrality, revolting against being mere objects, becoming stakeholders, taking part in the narration, almost stretching out their tongues and speaking, even reaching out their hands to scribble on my manuscript!'

'Was the scorpion-tattoo girl a Jew?'

'I don't know . . . honestly, I don't care. I know that she was from Paris but the tourists that come to that hotel are from all faiths, all countries. Sure, the hotel belongs to French Jewish investors but I don't know . . . she didn't speak Arabic and I don't speak French, so English it was. My English is poor: my school years were turbulent, without the chaos of the Intifada and the cheating on secondary-school exams in those days, I wouldn't have gotten into university.

'Afterwards, I did wonder about her being Jewish and ran through different scenarios. I asked myself why she hadn't left a trace or tried to come back. Was it the relationship itself that happened fleetingly like that or "my woman" had wanted it that way? Had she been a Jew who knew what an Arab was, one of those daughters of the colonizers who had a deep-rooted primitive impulse to domineer the colonized? But she was young, far too young . . . I dismissed that scenario. I don't even know how she chose me. I used to work opposite the pool. Had she noticed me there during the day? That night she arrived from the direction of the pool, as if she were going for a dip but then thought better of it. It was a wonderful experience for me, and that's that. I don't care about her religion—it's her scorpion that has nested itself in my imagination, just like the space between the two red lines drawn with her lipstick on the mirror.

'The hall was blown up and soldiers reoccupied the small cantons that they had partially left after the Oslo Accords (on that day I was in the village as I already said) and perhaps they destroyed the stairs of the dwelling where I had wanted to write my novel.'

*

'Coming back to my "crisis" with the hall. Now let me ask you a specific question, so that you'll understand me better and maybe I'll get you and myself a bit more, too: can a prisoner ever like his prison? This shack here that you sleep in is like a cell,' I said.

'Like my prison? How can I like my prison?'

'I'm not talking about prison as an antithesis to liberty, I mean "the place" itself, those square metres that you existed in for eighteen years, the wooden borsh planks that you sat on all those years, the walls that you brushed up against and that brushed up against your breath.'

'When you put it that way, maybe . . . but prison is still a prison. Far from what people think, I liked my prison in that it was a window to freedom. After I was freed, at times reality hit me hard, making my forehead bleed. At those moments, it's possible I had on rose-tinted glasses, remembering how you were the master of your own destiny, of that small world full of ideals, the internal system that you determined and defined with others. But you remain aware of what it all means, time passing you by because of prison, the way in which the bars steal your time by limiting your space in this universe to a couple of metres. In prison, over the long years, nearly all of yourself dies, in a manner more complicated than having a leg cut off and thrown away. When most of your self dies, life moves on, leaving a large part of you behind. Prison is more painful than having a limb cut off, or the destruction of stairs to a house you love or the sand of a scorpion tattoo crunching under your fingertips.

'When you return from this partial death to the whirl-wind of life, you don't understand much, and maybe you won't ever understand unless you have a crazy energy for life and freedom. You require great flexibility of mind to over-come it. Personally, I haven't missed my prison even for one day—maybe I've remained a prisoner to many things, but I haven't replaced my prison with other prisons, and I don't accept prison remaining in me.

'In prison, you like the dream of escaping, you nurture it like a scorpion trying to draw on a slippery mirror, you raise and protect it, even if it means digging your way out with a spoon. You long for small victories over your jailers, even if the victory is just looking at them in the eyes. But prison is filthy and those wooden planks, the borsh, are the worst things there are. People have varying degrees of sensitivity, and there are differences in how freedom is experienced, even among animals.

'When a place oppresses a person, he adapts, forgets, but then always ends up remembering again. The place moulds him, even if sometimes he can "fix" his mind.

'I'll tell you two stories about how a place overpowers. One of them happened to me, you'll see how a place oppresses the body, how it shapes it, not far off from how it comes across in your stories, or at least how I've understood it: the game of emptiness and fullness, reality and its representations, and how their roles switch in thinking and living. Once I tried to escape from prison. I hatched a plan with another prisoner that nearly paid off. We worked in the kitchen and were responsible for unloading the supply van. We were meant to escape in the van after overpowering the driver and his partner, but we were found out because it was a crazy idea. Sure, we overpowered both men, but how would we escape and where to in an occupied country? This was in the central Nablus prison. They caught us and we thought there wasn't much else they could do to prisoners already sentenced to life, but they decided to punish us with shackles. The penalty was for two entire years, our feet tightly bound with chains that stopped you from taking a step more than 10 centimetres long—I'm telling you the exact number because, over there, numbers have a meaning of their own, a taste rather, a smell, a touch. With chains like those, how you view distances becomes concentrated, forcefully compressed. It takes time to fully understand it, requiring extended thinking and deep reading.

'The shackles were so tightly bound that you had to take more than ten steps to cover a metre. This went on for two years. After they removed them, I walked. "Faster!" a prison guard yelled, laughing so hard he coughed. Only then did I understand I was walking, as if the chains had never been taken off. I couldn't escape from the restraints even though the iron was no longer there, it remained deep-rooted in my mind.

'The guard yelled a second time, delighted with my stumbling on "nothing", my stumbling on the shadow of the chains, or its ghost, or its emptiness if you prefer. Other guards joined in making fun of me, guffawing for a long time. To them it was as astonishing as it was ridiculous, but how painful it was for me, how much it made me understand, how much it deepened me. For weeks, every time I woke up, I started by taking half steps.

'How your father's leg hurts me, my friend! If my feet got so used to the shackles, what about a leg that has always been part of the body and is then amputated?

'They kept making fun of me for weeks—sometimes I even made fun of myself and my fellow inmate in chains.

'How your father's leg hurts me, just like the emptiness of your stairs that your friend stumbled on. Tied up by the emptiness, the emptiness of the removed shackles, I kept stumbling on it. How your scorpion hurts me, your many emptinesses hurt me like an imaginary shackle, oppressing and paralysing me.

'Now for another story with many heroes and Negev prison as the setting. The prisoners' exercise time was confined to a site 20 metres long, where the prisoners would walk every day for two hours, coming and going. At the end of the yard were rolls of barbed wire. If you bumped into them, you'd find yourself disfigured or, worse, disabled. So they took extra care on that end, turning round in the opposite direction as soon as they reached it. With time, prisoners got used to automatically turning around after exactly 20 metres without even looking at the fence or seeing it. More surprising, when an inmate left the prison, for a while things would be confusing; whenever walking in the street or in an open area, after 20 metres he would turn on his heel and double back in the opposite direction.

'Once a friend of mine went to congratulate a prisoner who had just been released from that prison, and when the two of them managed to get some distance away from those who had shown up, they spoke of politics and exchanged messages from between the prisons. Suddenly the prisoner started, his eyes fixed on the horizon. 'What? Did you just run into the fence?' my friend asked.

'You said it.'

The barbed wire was no longer there, but its emptiness remains stuck on your horizon, a barbed void that keeps you at a distance, separating you from him, and now separates you from yourself. That's prison for you.'

'And how about a prisoner liking his jailer?'

'Not a stupid question at all,' he said with a sense of confidence that came across as exaggerated. 'In my experience, the jailer fears being bewitched by the prisoner. Not all prisons are the same, not the jailers, not the prisoners. Prisons in this time of occupation are especially complex... it's not easy to snatch away the cause from a prisoner fighting for their freedom, his refusal to give in wears out the jailer.

The jailer assassinates your time, but you don't have to work to maintain your identity as a prisoner, while the jailer grows weary because he can't remove the mask of power, even just a bit, from his face to look you in the eye. He's afraid of sympathizing with you.

'So that you understand me, because it seems you've never been imprisoned (but who among us has never been imprisoned?), it's a bit like your work in the reception hall. You were able to fall in love with a girl there, or start a relationship without a hitch, even if she was Jewish. But I've always wondered about the young soldiers stationed at the Surda roadblock—how they look at the beautiful Birzeit university students. Does the soldier dare to look into the eyes of a girl he likes, forgetting the weight of the gun in his hands? It's tough. It'll awaken the human inside him! How can a soldier like that dream about a Palestinian girl, other than raping her—really, how? It's something like that between a jailer and a prisoner, with some shades of difference.

'Now, in cases of long imprisonment, the prisoner starts to feel his jailer changing and often this becomes his oxygen. A lot of the time the jailer stops paying attention to his mask and a sort of alchemy sprouts, a human alchemy, peeping out from the cracks of his human and moral weakness, as well as the vanity of his personal project.

'Maybe the gaze of a jailer for his prisoner is full of hatred that he's sheltered behind, but the gaze of a prisoner to the jailer is one of disdain. Disdain is sterner stuff than hatred. You're able to grasp this chemical equation without difficulty because your humanity is still breathing, and because you don't stand there like a jailer, watching over your freedom to protect it from yourself. Whoever has lost their humanity is no longer able to detect inhumanity in others. Power, so that it doesn't devour itself, requires great sensitivity towards weakness,' concluded the 'prisoner'.

## 8

## THE SCORPION'S FOURTH DANCE

It was in a hospital in Baghdad, in the final days of 2001. His terrifying yowl was the first thing I heard the moment I stepped into the surgery ward. There was a group of poets, whom I accompanied as a journalist; we were taking part in the Merbad poetry festival. During our trip, we went to the hospital to visit a group of those injured in the Intifada, people farmed out by the Arab countries for varied reasons including loyalty, propaganda, powerlessness, impudence; a large share of them were in under-siege Baghdad. The hospital that day was empty except for a handful of indispensable doctors, as everyone else had left following the order of the 'party' to attend a parade of a million soldiers of a popular army that went by the name Jerusalem. This army, it was said, was specifically for Jerusalem's liberation. That same day, Saddam Hussein—who was executed during the writing of this novel—inspected it for many hours, holding a heavy rifle in one hand while firing shots skyward.

It was wet and cold; the soft drizzle cleansing Baghdad didn't stall the parade. The young man was screaming. Our guide M., a Palestinian born in Iraq to refugee parents, seemed quite embarrassed. He didn't want the young man screaming, even after learning the nature of his injury, because on the smooth TV screens Palestinians were heroes; he mustn't sully that heroism even a little bit—never should a Palestinian cry in front of people!

We entered the room where the yelling was coming from. He was writhing on the bed, pleading with the doctor to give him something for the pain. Refusing outright, the doctor said another dose would ruin his stomach, necessitating another operation, which his body couldn't cope with. 'It's really hurting,' he continued to plead, 'the tips of my toes are itching, it's horrible, please make it stop, doctor!'

He cried, begged, while we looked on speechless at what he was gesturing to, where it was itching: emptiness was all there was . . . emptiness. They had cut his leg off that very morning just above the knee. But how was the foot of his cut-off leg itching him? Not able to curb my curiosity or the questions I'd stored away since my father's leg, I called the doctor to one side. 'Is it true what he's saying?' I whispered. 'Is the cut-off leg itching?'

'Yes,' he answered. 'For a certain period of time, the brain continues to emit signals that it has grown used to, so it'll take some time.'

It was the first time I'd heard a medical explanation, even partially, that something can feel like it needs itching even if it's not there. The few sentences that my father said in my presence on the day of his amputation came to mind.

'I woke up from the anaesthesia and saw it hanging in front of me. (He used the third- person pronoun, the pronoun for absent things, without naming it; only much later did I realize the rhetorical depth of using this pronoun.) I lost my mind and fell into a coma again. I woke up to see it a second time and lost consciousness again. After that, when I finally woke up, I begged the doctor to take it away from me. He told me I've got to see it to believe that it's no longer there, and that it would help me.'

Now after all this time, I find myself in Baghdad in front of a young man from Gaza, whose leg has been lopped off because of a serious injury, learning things I didn't know about amputation. The scene stayed with me from that day on: a young man in his late twenties, healthy, seemingly athletic, solidly built, whose leg had been cut off.

White gauze, wrapped above his left knee, and below it an emptiness, an emptiness that irritates and itches him.

If it were just me, I might have stepped forward and scratched the bottom of the emptiness; if it had seemed natural in such circumstances, I would have done it.

I was confident in that moment that I was completely capable of touching the edges of his emptiness, capable of distinguishing between the creases on the sole of his foot and the curves. I would have even held the toes and pulled them one by one, cracking them each in turn. After his amputation, my father's cut-off leg remained present in his imagination, whereas I constructed his amputated leg in my mind piece by piece until it became real.

I couldn't bear what I was seeing. We stepped out, my poet friend and I, to cry in the hospital's back garden; we cried bitter tears.

The weather was cold, Baghdad was melancholy, the rain gently coming down and the Iraqi palm trees crying. There were also pine trees (at least they looked like pine trees—I couldn't be sure). The young man continued to yell within me for a long time, his itching stuck in my mind; my hand ready to spring to scratch his emptiness, and now it's like I'm scratching it with my words. Isn't writing, in some way, the scratching of something that exists and doesn't exist at the same time? Something we know, we feel, we try to touch, to grasp, to silence? Isn't writing in some way a scorpion trying and trying to scramble up a mirror, to stop at a point, on some image, in some mind? Isn't that writing?

M., the young man, rejoined us, still embarrassed by the Palestinian who had cried, because his leg had been cut off.

We left, and saw a bit of the million-soldier parade, visited souks out of A *Thousand and One Nights*, ate masgouf made with a fish called Al-Qattan from the Euphrates. That day or the day after, we visited many monuments, including the Babylonian Lion—a massive black stone lion that the four marble lions of Al-Manara square always remind me of—I don't know why I hadn't really studied the Babylonian's Lion's features; I've always felt that I should have really examined them.

That day we visited a palace someone told us was one of Caliph Haroon Al-Rashid's, an absolutely magnificent edifice in which a delicate-minded friend forgot himself; he started knocking on the palace door, calling out, 'Open up, Zubeida, open up! It's me, Haroon!' With the utmost seriousness he exclaimed this, waiting for a response. It took a good few minutes for him to wake up from his 'dream'.

'It's as if I'm walking through the pages of a novel!' he claimed.

Our delicate-minded friend lost himself in the text; he was so deeply immersed in his reading of Iraq, especially the Abbasid period that he no longer knew where he was.

Three days in Baghdad. M. was with us, having volunteered to accompany us to smell the scent of Palestine on us, or so he said. Like a shadow he trailed us, never tiring, grumbling or asking us for anything. But whenever he was alone with me, he asked me to help him go back, as if it were the most obvious thing. More than once he asserted that he didn't want anything else; that he'd do any sort of work in Palestine—he didn't want a civil- servant post or any privilege despite being a member of the PLO. I couldn't figure out how serious he was; everyone knew that a refugee returning, whether to the lands occupied in '48 or those in '67, was nothing short of miracle. And he was closely tied to the political and diplomatic goings-on in Baghdad. I would respond diplomatically, sometimes confused; he would be silent.

We would pass the night at Mansour Hotel, one of the largest hotels in Baghdad. It was run-down, the signs of siege and poverty clearly visible: rusty taps, poor service and the TVs in our rooms only broadcasting Iraqi channels.

Our final night we stayed up: poets, writers, creative individuals. M. was with us as well as one the supposedly 'crazy' men—Majnoun—one of the Iraqi intellectuals. Majnoun didn't know fatigue. He talked about himself and his madness, about his game with madness, the madness of creativity and the creativity of madness. He read to us and us to him, it was a once-in-a-lifetime night.

That night I learnt how much madness could be one of the faces of reason, how much madness could be a mask and what it meant to need madness as a mask, when society's mind is closed off to the point that there is no other survival mechanism for a rational being.

But that's another story. Coming back to M., M. who read aloud to us while downing pints of arak. He would drink, imploring us to take him with us, begging and crying, 'Take me, I'll carry your bags, I'll work as your minder, I'll be your driver, I'll work as a sweeper, I want to go back with you all.' The more he talked, the worse he got; we pleaded with him, and tried to calm him down.

He would try and try and try, a dozen times (to convince us!) until, overcome with fatigue, until he dripped sweat, he fell down, flung onto his back, frothing at the mouth, moving his head and limbs with a desperate slowness, movements almost seemingly mechanical, as if they were his last.

The next morning he seemed fine when he came down to bid us farewell in the hotel's courtyard. The driveway leading to the main road from the hotel's entrance was lined with drawings of the American flag and photos of Bush Senior that were trampled either by those entering the hotel or exiting it. Flowers were in the courtyard, as well as a beautiful fountain. M. called me to the side saying, 'Listen, you set me at ease, you seem like a good person, understanding. I trust you and really want you to help me. Take me with you, take me with you, and I'll work as your minder, I'll carry your bags, serving you till the end of my days. Take me with you, I don't want my girls to grow up here, take me with you!'

His request tore me apart, making me feel small. I couldn't even argue with him, his hope lodged in my mind like the irritation of a cut-off leg needing to be scratched, just like the hereditary scratching of an ancient familial male tradition, like a call hanging suspended in the Baghdad sky, a sincere call to Zubeida, Caliph Al-Rashid's wife in this October of 2001.

## 9

## OTHER EMPTINESSES
## THE SCORPION ENTICES

I woke up optimistic; had a pot of locally made laban with a small piece of bread to relieve my stomach from the heartburn that had become a boring winter guest. The weather was sunny and beautiful. My long, sleepy morning daze was interrupted by a noisy notification from my mobile: a small transfer (from one of the Arab newspapers I used to write for under a pen name) had just arrived in my bank account.

It was noon. I left my place for downtown Ramallah: a lazy city full of potholes. Potholes on the roads, potholes in life, potholes in minds.

I went to the bank but was surprised to find it closed. I then remembered the directive for banks to close two days a week, as if we needed any more days off! I went to the ATM and came to know from those standing in the queue ahead of me that the banknotes I wanted had run out. Despite this, and because I had decided to make like an ostrich to the day's bad luck, I stayed standing in line, waiting my turn for the

ATM to tell me itself that the banknotes I wanted were not available.

The bearded oaf standing behind me further stoked my frustration by asking me a series of impossible questions that could be included, easily, among things divinely concealed. Didn't I think that the money he wanted would run out before he reached the ATM? And if the answer was yes, would he find what he needed at another ATM? With curt nods I answered, but my patience ran out when he asked me without any preamble or justification if I thought Abu Mazen would dissolve the Hamas-led government or not. 'I don't think Abu Mazen himself knows the answer to that one,' I snapped so sharply, it shut him up.

I kept standing in line for the ATM planted on the narrow strip of pavement at the Al-Manara Roundabout. More than one person tripped over me, some of them apologizing and others not. I accepted the apologies of some who made excuses, but for the most part I met their apologies with my depressed silence.

When the ATM confirmed, with its formal words of apology, the unavailability of the money that I already knew wasn't there, I walked a quarter of an hour to another ATM in 'Lower Ramallah', and when I inserted my card, the machine told me—what eloquence!—that my card had expired. You need a lot of bad luck for your five-year-old card to expire on the day the banks are closed, the card that was working just fine fifteen minutes ago, on top of how the ATM screen told you that the money you need isn't available. What pathetic plot lines, Mr Narrator!

Despite all this, I persisted with my original 'project' that I had left my place for: buying new leather flip-flops with the change left in my pocket. I'd ruined (for the thousandth time) my new flip-flops after I forgot to swap them for plastic ones when showering. Once in there, they drank up water till drunk, and soon enough smelt unbearable.

I headed back in the direction of Al-Manara Square. I examined the four lions, looking at them in a different light. These lions had changed, changed a lot. I drew closer and contemplated them as an admirer would . . . I love those lions. In the mid-50s, lookalikes of them were installed at the centre of the Al-Manara Roundabout, only to then be hidden away due to wars and lack of stability. But then, during the 'Oslo Spring', when change was in the air, they were replaced with new versions. The war broke out shortly after.

Often, I've heard people hoping to remove them temporarily again, but thankfully no one has done that; they've become part and parcel of us. What's the use of lions in storage? Why shouldn't we face our fate together? With this war, I feared for them, began to love them more, coming to know them by heart; I spotted them right away on TV and across newspaper pages—because they're at the heart of all news. All news.

The lions' smooth bodies have indiscriminate grooves left behind by bullets from confrontations that I only just noticed today. I've been tense, perhaps ever since they lost their tails, as the lions' tails, which weren't sculpted as lying flush with their bodies, were destroyed—specifically, the tail of the lion facing east, and that of the one facing west as well those of *its* lioness and two cubs. The tails plastered to the massive bodies perched on the massive stone plinth didn't suffer any damage.

What pulled me to the lions and strengthened my bond with them was the emptiness, the emptiness left behind by the amputated tails. Often, I've contemplated the emptiness, stared at it, got lost in my staring. I tried to dream of the emptiness some more, I felt it, and in it I sensed the emptiness of my father's amputated leg. I tried to grasp it in all its dimensions, to grab onto something in it, and all my emptinesses came rushing back.

I remembered the stairs and the dwelling itself after the landowner had wiped them from existence. I made my way towards the nearby parking lot where I would write my novel in the empty space between the two yellow lines on the black asphalt. I stared at the emptiness left behind by the dwelling on the second floor; it was suspended in the air, held up by the pegs of memory, the sit-downs and dialogues continuing. The emptiness that once had been occupied by the room wasn't like an emptiness that had never been occupied.

It's as if we were there, 'the great author' holding forth with great zeal, inspired by knowledge, creation, language; like a river he gushed forth—talking, dancing, gesturing with his hands. Often, his hands knocked against his glasses while wildly gesturing. His glasses fell while I looked at them, but the emptiness didn't catch them—they fell down, clattering against the parking lot asphalt.

I bought the flip-flops and returned to the lions.

I contemplated the lions some more, noticing a round stone watch engraved onto the paw of the lion facing east, its band on the back of the paw, the body (of the watch) on the inner wrist. The watch was stuck at 6.17 and one second exactly. Why this time in particular? Did it mean something to the sculptor? When he finished, for example? Maybe.

Scorpion, scorpion, scorpion. I became aware of the 'scorpions'—the hands—of the watch, scorpions of flesh and blood, my scorpion tattoo. What was the link?

Why did the sculptor stop the time? And why had he chosen that hour? Was it just random? What is this moment in time, which in his mind merits to be chiselled onto the lion's paw? Was it the end of a love affair or the beginning? Or when he finished sculpting?

No one can figure out what the sculptor had in mind.

The 'scorpion' of the watch leads me to another moment in the head of another person from Scorpion Land. Whenever he would come across me on my way to the dance hall or from it, he would stand and stop me, asking in stern Hebrew, 'Excuse me, what's the time?' On every occasion I'd answer him precisely, never feeling weary or that I was repeating myself.

'Then I'm late, very late indeed,' he'd say with the same sternness, with the same emphasis on getting the syllables out.

Logically, after learning the time and proclaiming his lateness, he should have sped up or changed his reaction at the very least. But no, this Hebrew would ask me and continue on his way at the same pace, his expression never changing.

I always think of him. He must have been in his fifties, somewhat medium-built, no distinguishing characteristics, his hair smooth, perfectly grey. He seemed distinguished but, in his severe elegance, like his language, I'd always felt a discordance, though I can't put my finger on it. Let's say that the well-pressed folds of his grey suit didn't chime with his body or features; as if his clothes were foreign to him or foreign to his taste. I wish I knew—just a hunch.

What was this man late for in Scorpion Land? What had the sculptor wanted by stopping the hands of time at 6.17? These questions continue to itch me without an answer to scratch them.

I remembered that I hadn't examined well enough the features of the black Babylonian Lion, so I looked closely anew at these lions of mine. The features of the lion wearing the watch seemed to emote a foolish contemplation, tinged perhaps with the idiocy of force, I don't know. The lion facing north was in a state of contemplation mixed with sadness, great sorrow. The one facing south was angry, furious in fact. The one looking west, flanked by the lioness and two cubs, possessed an anger that was something of a warning, a cautionary anger, perhaps because he was watching over a lioness and two cubs. I also noticed that the lioness was unusually small, only half the size of the lion; I don't know if the difference is a reflection of reality or an error on the sculptor's part.

The war didn't stop; neither did the afflictions of these lions. Beautiful lions, necessary despite the risks. Beautiful beasts, with the exception of the ridiculous iron structure that surrounded them. Many artists protested against it, yet no one listened to them. If this war wasn't on, if things weren't so tough, I swear—or as hapless in love 'Hallouq' says: 'I've got to divorce all the women on earth!'—I would organize demonstrations, marching at the head of them until this silly scrap of iron would be removed.

I kept on staring at the emptinesses. A blue car whizzed by, its driver yelling at a young man walking in front of me, 'Three were killed today! Do you know who?'

'None of them were ours.'

I then understood that they were talking about Palestinian refugees in Iraq, because the person driving the car was a visual artist come back from Iraq. I had seen him up close during one of his exhibitions.

I remembered M., his curious scorpion-esque dance, his intense pleading; I remembered the Babylonian Lion and its absent traits; I remembered Haroon Al-Rashid's Zubeida who didn't respond. The seller of sweet ringed bread next to me cried out, 'Kaak for sale . . . kaak for sale!' and yelled a prayer of Adel Imam's from the 'Leader' satire, 'Oh God, undress us and dress them!' I turned round to face the seller who had caught my attention with the eloquence of his language, and discovered his yelling was to harass two beautiful girls passing by, their attire not leaving much to the imagination.

I kept on observing and recording everything, like a camera snapping shots. Posters, slogans and declarations stuck to the lions' bodies and their bases, caught my attention: washed out, timeworn posters, others new and torn; declarations, notices and calls; I recorded them all letter by letter:

There is no G— | **Yout–** | Mohammed Tal | ... **DIRTY TRAITORS** ... | ... *from the Al-Am'a region* ... | ... **the prattling of the enemy of Islam** | IN THE NAME OF GOD THE MOST M— | ... the announcement ... | ... *with pride* ... | ... its martyr | ... aware of his reality ... | ... for a society ... | ... TO ANNOUNCE THE DEATH OF THE MARTYR'S BRIGA— | ... **MY** | **Arafat** | ... **AM** ... | ... were killed in defence of God | ... three

## 10

## A SOMBRE TUNE
## REVIVES THE SCORPION'S MEMORIES

2 February 2007

A soft rain washes the four Al-Manara Lions, their marble glistening. Many posters' words have been blotted out by the rain, rain washing the emptiness of the amputated tails, water running into the street streaming down the stone foundations.

I walked a little and stopped in front of the parking lot, umbrella in hand; impossible to sit there today. The parking lot attendant sells a ticket from his booth to a client. This young man has never understood me despite my peaceful 'parking'—regular and lucrative—he remains hostile towards my curious sitting in the emptiness between the two yellow lines. He doesn't take me seriously, even though I'm not hurting anyone.

The rain washes the parking lot tarmac, the asphalt looking blacker and the lines yellower too. Drizzle rinses the emptiness of the room suspended in my memory, and the emptiness of the six amputated steps.

Drizzle, bodies rushing, trickling rainwater gutters, the aroma of shawarma.

Catching sight of me, the young man gesticulates, calling out, 'Sir! Sir!' I approach, standing in front of the counter window.

'Where have you been? They arrested your friend a few days ago. He called this morning, and he'll call again on my mobile this evening—he wanted you to come here so he could talk to you or you can leave him your number, he's in Ofer prison, they've got contraband phones in there.'

It's the first time the boy speaks to me kindly, as if the imprisonment of our common friend makes him feel a sort of kinship with me.

'That's fine,' I say. 'I'll drop by this evening.'

'Something else sir, a question I've had for a couple of weeks—did you become a mirror?'

'What do you mean, have I become a mirror?'

'The first time you came here, you said you were trying to become a mirror. Did you succeed?'

'I hope I've succeeded, I hope so,' I responded smiling. I make my way towards the lions, thinking of my friend 'Revolution Mule'. What could have landed him back in prison at this age?

The sound of the rebab steals through the lazy, chaotic din, a sound that for years has been part of the city, drawing me in as I stand here, I hear it too from my transient parking lot 'office'.

The rebab is on the verge of disappearing and along has come this fifty-year-old man, of wheat-coloured complexion, to revive this old instrument on the pavements of a city propelling itself, somewhat floundering, to modernity. For years the man has been sitting daily on a plastic stool, hugging a rebab (that he had made himself I found out), making it croon, with two or three other rebabs next to him, on one of them a cardboard sign with the price: 10 dollars. The seller-musician switches between pavements depending on the sun: in winter, he follows its warm rays when they peek through the clouds; in summer, he follows the shade. Sometimes he plays because he feels like it, other times it's to attract a customer who took note of his strange instrument.

I always ask myself, who buys a rebab these days? The deserts that stay up at night to its melody are no longer deserts; the villages are no longer villages.

I imagine those who take notice of the rebab seller, and his music, are few and far between. Tourists are attracted by the strangeness of the tune and what the instrument looks like. Me, I'm pulled in by it for different reasons; several times I've meant to buy one, but keep putting it off. The rebab's string is what gets me: one solitary string (just like me), a horsetail string caressed by another cord made taut by a bowed almond branch.

No brother you have, rebab cord, no brother have I. The nay is like us, it has one cord, a cord of air. The nay's cord is its emptiness. I remember Hussein Barghouti's poetry, 'I'm not a nay, I'm the emptiness within it.'

So it's the emptiness, emptiness once more and the empty spaces in front of me washed by the drizzle. And the rebab seller plays a tune I don't know that pulls me by the collar of my soul to my mountain, to my father's emptiness, to our cave, Mountain Gob, the cave of Saadi the shepherd: saved from certain death by his rebab's melody on a moonlit spring night at the start of the twentieth century.

The story goes: one spring, Saadi was with his flock in 'mountain gob'. During the day he would lead his sheep to graze in the mountains, and at night the cave would shelter him. Out in front of the cave was a pen, made of row upon row of stone with firewood on top, where the sheep would spend the night. The darkness of that time was lit up by the moon and wicks soaked in petrol lamps that went out early; people slept a little after the sun set and woke up just before it rose.

Saadi's nights were of the moon, of bells, of sheep and goats. His days were herding his flock and his rebab.

The shepherd had an intelligent sister named Widadi, who would spend the night in their wooded shack in the village (my village) on a small hill at the foot of the mountain.

Saadi was fast asleep (no better sleeper than him, many a storyteller said). Wearing the mask of night, of darkness, of solitude, of silence, they came to his cave, intending to kill him. The smell of their weapons subdued his dogs' barking. He implored them to give him a chance to play a final tune on his rebab, and talked of slaughtering one of his rams to grill on the pen's firewood.

Enticed by the idea of grilled meat, they slaughtered the ram and began to eat after barbecuing it. As Saadi played his final tune, Widadi heard her brother's melody from the bottom of the mountain, understanding his message. She sought help from the village dwellers, their houses close enough to touch one another. With a few weapons and sticks, everyone responded to the call. The shepherd was saved and the village now had a story to pass down for generations. A tale of pride, glory, and a melancholy tune that goes like this:

Oh Widadi, oh Widadi
They killed your brother Saadi
Killed the goat

*Grilled his flesh on the fence*
*Widadi your brother is gone*
*The soil his blood spilled on*
*Gather the beds of celebration*
*Cover your face with soot.*

Children of the village, and those right after, and the generations to come, heard the tale from their little hill, facing the giant mountain and its open cave that looked like a lion's mouth in mid-yawn. They all would listen to the tale from 'below', imagining the cave and the mountain in front of them. I'm the only one whose consciousness awakened in the cave and around it; I used to hear the tale while perched on Saadi's very spot. A world of difference when picturing the story from one place to another.

He played a tune about the thieves that nearly killed him and stole his flock, standing atop a mountain that looked like the giant stage of a legendary theatre, an open theatre, whose audience was the people, the plains, the mountains— reaching to the sea.

Saadi played his melody alone, the melody descending freely, fairy-like, to the sea and beyond. I went down one day to the sea, not a fairy-like descent, nothing like the melody. I went down in a bus, one like the thousand others that for years had been collecting men from the mountain villages and cities at the end of the night to sow them on the shore of the Mediterranean. They were then gathered back up in the afternoon, seeds at nightfall brought back to the villages to lay their heads down to sleep.

*

Where have you taken me, rebab man? And you, drizzle? Your melody is forlorn today, or could it be my friend's imprisonment pulling me down? Is the sad lion facing the north tearing up, or is it just raindrops?

Raindrops or tears? Can an eye of stone cry?

The tears dragged me back to my mother's eternal tears, when she would hold my hand and take me down the mountain. A glacial breeze would whip our faces, making golden hair dance, hair that would one day entice the young waitress at the entrance to the lift in Scorpion Land to comb her fingers through its tresses without so much as a warning. That was before she served in the army; after that, she changed.

Her army was overburdened with iron; mine was of dreams.

My hair was a story all on its own; my mother let it grow for her own reasons. She realized my beauty was bewitching and wanted to chase away the evil eye, so she let it grow, as she so often said with me around. She plaited it so everyone would think I was a girl, because who would envy a village girl? Only sons were worth envying!

As a child, my mother wanted my hair long; an amulet to chase away jealous eyes, like the many blue beads fastened with pins to my clothes (according to the photos).

When I joined school, they shaved my head. It was shocking. After that, never did I get my hair cut at a barber's without him saying the same thing, as if all barbers had agreed on it beforehand, 'What a shame, believe me, it's not easy for me to cut this hair and throw it on the ground, this is gold, your hair is pure gold!'

Tears in my mother's eyes, tears in eyes of stone . . . tears in the sockets of plucked-out eyes.

More than once I told my aunt while she was spinning stories, 'How can a girl with plucked-out eyes cry?' She would swat the air and smile faintly, 'Do you want me to keep talking, darling? That's how the story goes!'

I loved my aunt and all her stories. As a child I'd always imagined her marrying 'Hallouq'—he who constantly shaved—and to this day I don't know why I chose him. He seemed suitable for her, better than her husband whom I hate, without even knowing him, what after he left her and went to America. I had always wished she would marry Hallouq instead. Hallouq the simple bachelor who couldn't find anyone to marry him. Despite this, whenever he lost his temper he never cooled down until he declared his famous and laughable oath, 'I've got to divorce all the world's women!'

Here's my aunt's story about the crying plucked-out eyes (as I remember it): there were three sisters, hungry and cold, huddled around the brazier in a small shack, each of them dreaming aloud and making wishes. The eldest wished that God would marry her to a butcher to feed her so much meat you'd only seen the likes of it in your dreams, or only ever tasted at weddings, and to give birth to a daughter who, with every word she spoke, a piece of gold would tumble from her lips.

The middle sister (less greedy) wished God would marry her to a baker so that she could eat enough bread to never go hungry again. As for the youngest, she wished for a lumber-jack to live with and would be happy with whatever he could provide.

It just so happened that night that the king was making his rounds, visiting his subjects, and heard the three sisters' modest dreams; he decided to make them come true without telling them. The next day he sent his soldiers to invite them to the palace. Terrified, the sisters kept pleading until they discovered what was going on. They then got married just as they had wished: the eldest to a butcher, the middle to a baker and the youngest to a lumberjack.

They all grew pregnant and gave birth: it was the oldest's fortune to have ugly girls, the middle sister's to have average-looking girls and the youngest, a beauty queen as a daughter. (My aunt recounted this sitting in bed, her bottom half and hands snug under the duvet on those winter evenings, and at this part of the tale she'd usually comment, 'Because your fortune, my sweet, depends on your intentions. The greedy elder sister, God didn't bless her, but look at the youngest, God told her, "take with both hands!"')

The news of her beauty reached the prince (the son of the king who had visited his subjects that night—and of course this prince lived in the city), so he sent his match-makers and his men to the lumberjack to bring him the girl, after giving her family whatever they wanted. Her father was honoured by this relationship by marriage, but he refused for his wife to accompany their daughter to the city. While bidding her farewell at the edge of the village, her greedy aunt volunteered to escort the girl with one of her own daughters; so they all clambered into the howdah together.

On the long journey (weeks long) in a caravan of camels, mules and donkeys, the bride-to-be got thirsty and asked her aunt for some water. She refused. After imploring and bargaining, the aunt demanded one of her niece's eyes for a sip of water. When faced with the choice between the fires of death or blindness, her niece did what had to be done; and at a later stage, her other eye was plucked out, too.

The aunt put both eyes in a box and threw the bride-to-be out of the travelling howdah after having taken her clothes. She dressed her own daughter in the bride's finery and made her up as best as she could (here my aunt usually noted that you can't even trust your own sister with your daughter, because jealousy will push her to do horrible things).

The bride-to-be, with eyes plucked out, sat in a garden in the middle of the road, crying. 'How can she cry without eyes?' I'd ask my aunt. She'd elude the question with a swat of her hand or unsatisfying answer, 'That's how the story goes dearest,' and carry on.

She cried and complained, and with every word she uttered, a pearl or a nugget of gold would tumble out. The owner of the garden arrived and saw the most astonishing sight: a pile of gold in front of a girl whose eyes were missing, and on her very shoulder grew wondrous and extraordinary flowers, unlike any other on the face of the earth. If picked, more would immediately sprout in their place, even more stunning.

The gardener took the girl in and came to know her story. He decided to retrieve her eyes. Snipping off the flowers at her shoulder, he put together an astonishing bouquet and went in front of the prince's palace, hawking the flowers, setting the price as a pair of eyes; strange flowers from Eden require a strange price. The aunt married to the butcher came out of the palace with her daughter. Failing to acquire the bouquet with a king's ransom in gold, the daughter (now the prince's wife) remembered that her cousin's eyes were hidden away in a box in the palace. Buying the bouquet, despite her mother's protests, the eyes were returned to their rightful owner. The lumberjack's daughter built a palace next to that of the prince and, upon seeing her, he realized the truth.

A lot of gold in poor people's stories, a lot of gold and princes, and beauty that simply grazes misery and poof it's gone; a lot of gold and princes owning everything.

Even the names in the tales of poor people throb with the dream of escaping poverty and hunger. No one knows how far back these stories go, but what I can't forget are the names; names of beauties whose appearance were reason behind a marriage of money and power. One of their names was 'Pearl Strings Gold Platters'; yes all of that is a name! And another, 'Tall Beautiful' . . . and they each have their stories.

In most of the stories, the solutions come from outside. Some prince loves a beautiful girl and solves the poverty problem—there's a barter system between beauty and power that I never liked, and I don't like this waiting for solutions from outside. The prince is nearly always the solution and not part of the problem. I had shared this with 'the prisoner' in our nightly chats before his imprisonment, and he said, 'I agree with you when it comes to waiting for change in the village from the outside, but I don't know if it's specific to the village or Arabs in general or all of mankind, but I remember a funny story from my village that backs up what you're saying, it goes back the '40s of the last century.

'A man came to the village riding a donkey, a dignified-looking man with a long beard. People welcomed him in the guesthouse of honour. When it was time for the sunset prayer, they took him to the mosque and insisted that he lead them in prayer. So he prayed, but did so in silence, whereas the sunset prayer is recited aloud, as everyone knows. He finished praying and instead of criticizing him, each of them said to the other, 'Praise be to God; year after year we've been going about this prayer all wrong, until this man came and showed us the right way.'

'One of the villagers hosted him for a few days, and the first chance he got, the guest stole everything in the house and took off!'

*

In the evening, I returned to my 'virtual office' at the exact stipulated time, and the 'freed prisoner' (who was no longer free) called me from Ofer prison, his voice distorted by an echo I couldn't figure out.

'How's the novel coming, friend?'

'Fine. What about you? Your news is more important. Has the "mule" gone back to work?'

'No, no, don't get me wrong, don't worry, it's nothing serious: I was in the north arranging for some rice and vine leaves (code name for ammunition that I understood from living through the first Intifada) for some young men, you know. They slaughtered them like chickens, that's all there is to it. What's important is your novel, how's the scorpion?'

'Fine. He sends you his best.'

'If I were you, I'd let him out so he could sting. . . .'

The garbled call got cut off, like a leg, his words resounding in my head.

What would I have said if the call hadn't been cut? I don't know. I wanted to tell him that my scorpion didn't sting, my scorpion was a handsome one, nice, delightful . . . I realized that I didn't know a thing about real scorpions; I thought I must read up about them so I could defend mine. I went to a cyber cafe and surfed; I discovered some extraordinary things:

*Its unchanging characteristics over the past 400 million years have been the essence of its survival. The scorpion has four sets of legs and a pair of small pincers to slice its prey.*

Eight legs for a scorpion and one for my father!

*There are 1,500 scorpion species worldwide, of which 50 are harmless to man.*

It seems like my scorpion belongs to this group.

*The scorpion's poison kills its prey and helps it digest.*

*According to the prophets, the scorpion is cursed, so killing it is permitted during the holy months.*

*A nocturnal carnivorous creature, with six to twelve eyes capable of fasting for three consecutive years. With no sense of smell or hearing, it depends on acoustic vibrations.*

*The gestation period for the female scorpion lasts from several weeks to a year-and-a-half. Over a period of twelve days she gives birth to her offspring, about thirty. Then for two weeks she carries them on her back, feeding them from her prey and then releases them . . . The scorpion uses its venom with great intelligence, never using it all up in one go or attacking humans under normal circumstances, unless it feels threatened.*

I kept perusing the websites and was content that I hadn't known a single thing about real scorpions before writing. It would have muddled up my mental scorpion, my dream scorpion—especially when I learnt of the scorpion's dance, a dance to seduce his female mate who would then devour him after impregnation, taking advantage of his exhaustion.

That's why it's called 'the dance of death'. My scorpion's dances were definitely not dances of death!

More about scorpions I found online: *Many of us believe and say that scorpions are generally deadly animals. Hollywood has perpetuated this stereotype with all of its scorpion films. But the truth that many do not know is that a scorpion's sting is similar to that of a bee. Only a small group of species have potent poison and they are generally not found in areas inhabited by humans. Scorpions without a harmful sting have found their way into American houses as pets.*

About the zodiac sign: *Among the strongest and toughest signs. On the outside, they appear calm and in control but strong emotions bubble underneath. They're like a volcano agitating under the sea surface. Whoever deals with them intelligently is able to discover the power, exuberance and hidden magnetism in their personality. At social gatherings, scorpions are poised, diplomatic and talkative and inspire joy.*

*The scorpion belongs to the phylum of arthropods and class of arachnids that includes scorpions, spiders and ticks, which are often found in hot regions, typically the humid ones. Many kinds exist, reaching up to eight hundred. Scientists don't classify them among insects as, in accordance with the classification mentioned above, they are animals.*

*When faced with critical danger such as fire, the belief that a scorpion will commit suicide appears to be a myth from the Middle*

East. *Scientific research shows that this notion is lacking truth: when exposed to extremely high temperatures, the scorpion is prone to agitation like any other creature, and tries to escape. This is apparent from the tail incessantly moving right, left, up and down. No longer able to fully control its tail, the scorpion may sting itself by mistake.*

# TWO CHARACTERS FROM
# THE SCORPION'S FAMILY

He came up to us on the mountain, leaning on his cane, arriving worn out. I had heard a lot about him, but rarely seen him; he was approaching sixty at that time (in the days when I left the mountain). In the cave, my father prepared coffee on a small stove that he usually kept in front of him the whole day along with coffee supplies, little flecks of remaining paint on its body showing it had been orange once upon a time.

My father handed the coffee to the guest, but he put it down in front of him, refusing to drink. No, I said to myself, it's not possible. All those years I had thought of how my paternal aunt hadn't married after her scoundrel of a husband had up and left her—me dreaming of her marrying this very man in front of us. Had he come today to ask for her hand, at this age? Refusing coffee usually was in the context of a big demand, nothing less than asking for marriage.

My thoughts didn't last long, my father sat up rod-straight from the temporary refusal of his coffee.

'Everything OK, Hallouq? Ask away.'

'Don't shut Mountain Gob. On the life of your only son, don't. Who knows, what it might say some day,' he said with a smile that even today is difficult for me to interpret.

'Drink your coffee and don't tell me to swear on my only son. For him, I'd tear out my own eyes right now and feed them to the birds. Hallouq, you're a friend, you know. I don't need to swear on my only son to give open-handedly, you know how generous I am.'

'I know, I've got to divorce all the world's women! Don't I know it. I'm sorry, I didn't mean to scare you, but I heard that you want to close off Mountain Gob with an iron gate and use it for yourself. I'd be lost if I looked to the mountain and didn't see the old man's mouth laughing, like he's done for the past hundred years. So I told myself I'd come see you, and here I am, you won't send me back disappointed.'

Just then his face grew heavy with disappointment as he said, 'Also, the people in the village made a bet . . .'

We were all seated at the entrance to the cave; my father roared with laughter, and so did I. Hallouq joined in, laughter streaming out of Mountain Gob that wouldn't be closed now after all, thanks to his meddling. The wadis and mountains responded with echoes of our unhinged laughter. While laughing, I took the chance to observe Hallouq's face: his chin and a side of his moustache were shaved, making for an excruciatingly off-putting image.

Hallouq's main tale (as he had many a tale) started in the village guesthouse, where some talk had taken place; those speaking weren't in accord when assessing the sequence of events. Some said that *this* would happen; Hallouq said *that* would happen and pronounced a popular oath used in the villages but that no one followed through with easily: 'If that happens, I'll shave off half of my moustache!' He challenged them all, and in the end they made him fulfil his oath, shaving one side off and leaving the other, for reasons too long to explain. From then on, his betting increased, whether of his own accord or spurred on by others; the bets became less important in nature, knotted in small circles for petty reasons. Things then progressed and Hallouq started to bet on victories that hadn't happened, on royal interventions that hadn't happened and on international decisions that hadn't been applied, things of that nature.

Hallouq's condition came to light in his childhood when he went to the city and entered the cinema. He said assalamu-alaikum and went towards the front row where he shook everyone's hand one by one until the rest of the audience took notice, and an alarming laughter rang out that he didn't understand. One of those whose hands he had shaken sat him down kindly.

This was just a simple example to understand the story of the perpetual missing demi-moustache, lost in bets, leaving behind an irksome emptiness on the tableau of his shaved face. An emptiness of this type is bothersome (usually) more than that of an amputated leg. The leg is a limb, it's clear that it's an extension of a centre and stops at a precise point. The emptiness of the missing stairs remains suspended between two remaining steps: one at pavement level and the other at the doorstep high above—it's an emptiness that one can grasp or conceive a sort of equilibrium for, but, on the tableau of the shaved face, the absence of half a moustache is weighty, its emptiness unbearable, an unsupported emptiness, an emptiness standing undecided on the edge of an abyss.

He wasn't an idiot (although he did have something of Dostoevsky's The Idiot). For some reason, he couldn't discern the masks in words; for him, shaving his moustache was shaving his moustache—things only had one meaning, immediate and direct. Many things proved to me that he was intelligent, brave and deep, drawing me towards him and making him a suitable choice, I thought, as my aunt's groom. The most present thing in my mind is that he remained the 'servant' of the guesthouse even after it was no more. Every night, people would take turns telling stories.

Once, one of the common folk asked to speak and it went like so: There once was a king with no money, no means. Laughter exploded in the guesthouse and comments rained down, 'A king with nothing?!' The bizarreness of the story's start became a story in itself, actually the entire story, as the audience stopped the story from going any further.

Only Hallouq stood up for the speaker, asking the audience to be quiet so the rest of the story could be heard. He tried, but the astonishment was overwhelming; the beginning of the tale deviated from the usual logic of storytelling. It was staggering and highly unlikely. The king conventionally owns everything, even the narrator and the characters themselves—in poor people's stories there is a lot of gold, princes who marry poverty and transform it into wealth.

When I think back on this now, I'm much more aware of the curse of storytelling, its restrictions, its mines, its pitfalls. I had always wanted to know the story of that king who didn't own anything, but how? Laughter silenced the tale, the marginality of the narrator making it lost forever.

Had Hallouq had enough of bets after making my father swear on me that he wouldn't shut Mountain Gob? It's possible, because he let on that he had told the gamblers, 'I'll make the bet, but on the condition that it's my last.'

I remain inhabited by Hallouq's tales and the emptiness of his moustache. His saying 'Don't shut Mountain Gob . . . who knows what it might say some day,' sinks deep down, settling at the bottom of my worlds.

On the mountain, my aunt was the 'dream lady'— dreaming, recounting and interpreting her dreams; people believed her, quite possibly, because she believed herself. Women started to come and share their dreams: secrets, bottled-up things, images. Women came recounting their dreams, their husband's dreams and those of their children. My aunt became a dream reservoir; I'd listen and draw much from her stores, as much as my consciousness allowed me.

Perhaps I was contaminated by her dream-like nature. Should I tell her my dream, the scorpion one? So often, I'd hoped to do so, but the intense sensuality of the story with the girl and in the reoccurring dream that followed it, complicated the matter considerably—but it's not just that. Now, when I go back to the mountain occasionally, things feel different, some threads torn apart, broken. I'm no longer myself, neither is my father, nor my aunt, nor the mountain.

I had wanted, for instance, to ask my aunt some details of the stories she had told me as a child, some of the things swirling round my head, but whenever I sat next to her, the circumstances didn't seem suitable at all. The questions that a child asks while listening to a story are understandable and justified, but a man asking about children's stories is out of place, or seems so.

The logic of childhood stories, their justifications, their atmosphere, are all part of the story. The child listens to them with the imagination of a child—the narrator, knowing his world, manoeuvres the narrative threads without any sentiment of responsibility. I felt that after a quarter of a century had passed since those nights, I would no longer be able to listen, nor would she be able to tell such stories.

My aunt rejoined our family just after my grandfather's death. She had been married for a year to a young man who took off for America and left her with a pile of beguiling promises that she quickly exhausted. She was slightly younger than my father, extremely intelligent. She hadn't completed her schooling after primary, as that was the final class offered in the village at that time (the boys would go on foot to nearby villages).

My aunt's network of female relations was astonishing; it followed her to the mountain. Perhaps this ascension to an isolated mountain gave the magic of her personality an added dimension. With the distance and the altitude, maybe the female visitors (or even my father's male ones) felt removed from the usual rules of disclosure within the societal fabric:

the women would talk, the threads of their stories reaching the spindle that my aunt held, threads she'd stitch into marvellous embroideries.

Threads of dreams leaving houses and neighbourhoods, entering others, maybe even crossing the village border to a nearby village. I would pick up many things, most certainly forming in me things I'm aware of and others that I'm not.

While the women shared their dreams, my aunt asked precise questions, sometimes nervous ones; the answers would be fearful, sometimes hesitant. Waiting for the interpretation of a dream was tough, a crucial exam: Was there blood in the dream? Blood dirties dreams. Your dead relative visited you; did he give you something, did you give him anything? Did you eat his food? You kissed your dead father's hand? It's OK, was it a moist or dry kiss? What was he wearing? Did you get in a car with him? Good heavens, a car means a funeral! You saw a plane? Ya lateef, that means a grand death, and the plane landed? Where did it land? You had a child at sixty? O God, what came out? Did the newborn speak? What did it say? Did you see teeth in its mouth? You walked barefoot in the road? Did you find your shoes?

Many dead people in those women's dreams; one of them visited a dead man, he invited her to sit down, all the chairs around him were smashed, missing their essential parts, making it impossible to sit down. 'Better that way,' my aunt said. In another dream, the dead clustered round enormous pots, steam and vapour rising from them—the pots turned out empty, no food or water in them.

It was a kingdom of dreams with her as the queen. They had absolute trust in her, and she didn't abuse it; by a certain age she grew bothered by my presence, to the point she banned me completely from eavesdropping on their conversations.

When I matured, learnt, tied the threads together and thought about it, it seemed that my aunt possessed an unmatched skill of interpreting dreams and dealing with them; aside from the fantastical creative and visionary dimensions of dreams, there's an information infrastructure that allows the understanding of fears and obsessions. Maybe my aunt held the essential keys to a complex map of love, hatred, envy and hidden intentions. But she would always nourish the good in her interpretations.

My listening scope narrowed when I became more aware; my ability to spy on this seductive world diminished, because of my aunt's loyalty to the women. They trusted her, telling her about their dreams and bodies, sometimes even submitting their bodies to her.

A few times, young women who has just given birth came to her, their newborns refusing to breastfeed for myriad reasons. These women were in pain from the build-up of milk. My aunt would place pieces of fabric soaked in I don't know what; other times she would suck at the nipple herself and spit out the milk.

Once, I was up quite close and they didn't notice me. A young woman had come with her mother, and in a moment laid bare her round, white, breast; my aunt approached, sucked it and spit several times. They were sitting on rock slabs behind our isolated home, with no onlookers to worry about in the solitude of the mountains. She would suck the milk and spit it out; it glinted, dribbling down the rock, the sun reflecting off the rock and the whiteness of the breast.

'Why don't you buy a suction pump?' my aunt asked. 'No one breastfeeds any more these days.'

'I didn't think of asking my husband.'

'Why don't you ask him to suck?' my aunt pushed, and collapsed in a fit of laughter with the young girl's mother.

The young woman chuckled as well. 'He's tried already,' she said timidly. 'But he didn't like the taste of my milk.'

Laughter rumbled once more. Suddenly, my aunt caught wind of my presence, staring at the round white breast, lit up by the sun, hungrily consuming the words smelling of milk. She rebuked me, so I moved away—this was all much later, but with great regret, it was the final time.

My aunt had a close relationship with the emptiness and its game, a different relationship belonging to her fantastical world, where she would treat warts with a ritual that seemed like a game of illusion. An old treatment, which after inquiring I learnt wasn't her invention, but that it was rather common, used by folk healers—but from one healer to the next, the method was poles apart.

Those with warts would come to my aunt; she'd ask them to arrive with an egg laid on a Saturday and a fig-tree branch. They would have to bury the egg in a pile of ashes on their way back home from our house, not speaking to anyone before reaching there. The branch, she positioned on a cutting board in front of her, grasped a sharp knife, placed it on a section of the branch and said to the afflicted individual, pointing to one of the warts, 'Look here, I'm cutting it. Take a good look, I've cut it off.' Then she'd move to the second and the third in the same manner.

She'd convince the patient that the warts had been cut off, not the fig branch cut up. She'd ask them to take the branch, now in pieces, and soak it overnight in moonlight. Three days to be fully healed is what she would determine, and that's generally what happened.

My father's 'real' leg was amputated; its emptiness and itching remained. My 'real' places had been splintered to pieces; their emptiness and the illusion of them remained.

But my aunt, she tore out warts with an illusion, pulled them out of the imagination, and they transformed into emptiness!

## (12)

## AT THE SCORPION'S BIRTHPLACE
## IS WHERE IT HAPPENED

She came to you, stumbling in her confusion. You found her heavy with desire.

How distant you are now, how clear! Eighteen years on, it's as if I'm seeing you with eyes other than my own, with eyes other than yours. I see you squeezed in Scorpion Hall, wearing a cerulean shirt with dark-blue horizontal stripes. I see you preparing tables for more than 250 guests, on your own, for nearly every day of the summer season, when events and parties abound.

I see you now, fleeing the suffocating love of your parents to fall into the embrace of drastic harshness, the harshness of life and exploitation. Your mother's teacher salary was enough, but you wanted to escape the image your parents had framed of you in their minds, only for you to fall into the trap of a distorted image in the minds of your employers.

You loved the sea, the mermaids and you wanted to learn about those you were battling with on the mountain. In a year, you will have devoured their language in such a way it astonishes them.

I see you now, waking up at six, collecting tablecloths from the party the night before; washing the floor; buffing the plates, glasses and spoons with a moistened rag, removing any dried water droplets until they shined; setting out clean white tablecloths and starting to set each guest's place: three plates—the large one, then the middle one and the smallest atop them all, two forks, a knife, a small spoon, a water glass and a wine glass. You fold the blue napkin in the shape of a flower and place it atop the three plates.

It's now 5.30 in the afternoon, everything is nearly ready—you make the platform's red carpet glisten with a moistened rag, its gleam completing the glitter of the hall. You retire from the stage, from the hall, to your eternal place: the kitchen. Even though you've just done more labour than two workers combined, you only take a half-an-hour break before launching into another round of gruelling work. It's time to receive the empty plates and prepare them for the dishwasher. Other workers, who work only part-time, join you: Arabs, Ethiopian Jews and Eastern Jews. Dance and song go on till two in the morning, leaving you with only four hours of sleep.

On stage, they sing songs that you don't understand in the first few months, but you quickly pick up on the meanings and make fun of them to yourself: a song where someone sighs as if planning a trip, his friend then asks, 'Where to?'

'The land of Israel,' he answers. Another song criticizes the government for raising taxes . . . such poor taste.

I see you, handsome, making off with the nickname 'Blondie' or 'Al-Janji' in Hebrew, in a country with no shortage of blondes. I see you, strong, the mountain having toughened up your body, toughened up your soul after standing alone on the precipice of nothingness. I see you, intelligent, having inherited your wits from your genius parents. I see you shifting things around, making observations on work arrangements to reduce costs and everyone's efforts.

On days with fewer events, I see you in a dark hall, sitting on the stage till the end of the night, only the lights above your head shining. You're reading and translating Hebrew newspapers as if you have an exam the next day, reading books bigger than yourself that you took from your father's library—that he never cracked open after his amputation. You read as if it wasn't you who couldn't bear school.

One evening, your supervisor comes to 'inspect' you; a fat, jolly man always with a joke, his eyes large and bulging, forever red from work and staying up late. He sees you walking on stage, memorizing something aloud. 'What are you reading there?'

'Something of Shakespeare's, a play called *Macbeth*.'

'Shakespeare, ah yes, Shakespeare!'

'You know him?'

'Yes, I know him! Listen, I got here, to the top of the hospitality and cooking world from nothing. I was abandoned in a "city of development", a humiliated Eastern Jew. I reached here, the centre: the most expensive, the richest and the highest place. Take my advice, if you want to live a good life, then work in food, people won't stop eating till Judgement Day, simply said, they'll never stop eating. There's always work in our field, what is life but food! Now don't forget we have a lot of parties next week. Make sure everything is as it should be. Look here, I've worked hard to get where I am, I'm a real success story—if only you knew how I lived at your age!'

A success story, yes. I was in solidarity with many aspects of his story, and didn't harbour any personal hatred for the man but I had known, and come to know even more with time, the terror of its collective fabric. A story that would have remained very much stagnant without my story or because of my story (my game, our game is a game of stories).

My supervisor left and I kept on acting, learning parts of *Macbeth* by heart. He was talking about his fear that the ghosts of the dead would return (my game, our game is a game of ghosts), trying to convince his wife that he wouldn't kill the king to seize power. The arrival of the king draws near and Lady Macbeth slips her final advice in his ear:

**LADY MACBETH**

> *Only look up clear.*
>
> *To alter favour ever is to fear.*
>
> *Leave all the rest to me.*

**MACBETH (alone)**

> *If it were done when 'tis done, then 'twere well*
>
> *It were done quickly. If the assassination*
>
> *Could trammel up the consequence, and catch*
>
> *With his surcease success; that but this blow*
>
> *Might be the be-all and the end-all here,*
>
> *But here, upon this bank and shoal of time,*
>
> *We'd jump the life to come.*

I see you, see myself quickly understanding things. The place suffocates you. I see you combining work in the hall and the hotel kitchen, sleeping in a shelter just for Arab workers (ten employees in the shelter). I see a beautiful, idiotic, bourgeois secretary calling you to an office of glass, a glimmering office: she stops you in front of her and asks you to dust the ashtray, within earshot of her friend on the other end of the line. The ashtray was already sparkling but she wanted to show her friend that she could give orders; this idiotic secretary (a specific type of idiot, what I call a bour-geois idiot). So you dusted and smiled bitterly.

She saw you in her present, you saw her in your future.

Small, ever so small, she appears in your future, just an idiot.

Your image was distorted in her mirror, really distorted compared to how you saw yourself in your own mirrors (because it's a game of optics, it's a game of mirrors).

That day you decided to change your trajectory, and went back on your decision to leave school, getting out of that context.

But you kept going back, in your memory, in your dreams. You drew so far away from yourself to the point it seemed you were no longer yourself!

I see you now with your first girl from far, far away, I see you both naked on the stage, I see a pretty lipstick drawing on a wall . . . a mirror. How different the drawing looks from afar, from her that you drew and saw on stage.

You dream of going back there, where you were a worker, you dream of switching places, of playing the tourist instead of the dishwasher, of others preparing everything for you. You discover your problem isn't with the work itself, but being stuck prisoner in a narrow, cruel framework that cramps your dreams and confines your potential.

You dreamt of telling the story after that. It fascinated you. You planned to go there, to write a chapter in the hotel, on the balcony of one of the rooms above the hall or by the swimming pool in front of it, luring the memories forth and looking at things with a new eye.

And then a war broke out. You wished it would keep its distance from Scorpion Hall; you always told yourself if something happened there, everything would be upended— your going back there would become more difficult, it would carry more significance than you would want to ascribe to it. You just wanted to go there to dwell on personal things, as far as possible from buried ghosts, grand stories and historical nightmares that had twisted the memory of the place.

A young man, one of you and your cause, came in and blew up the place, with your friends and colleagues inside. If you had been at the entrance, would you have grabbed his hand and tried to convince him to go back or let him settle his own accounts? You don't know. Not because you're schizophrenic, but because the schizophrenia of the place was greater than you! You had tried to dodge and keep your story at bay, but the place took you by storm and threw you off kilter.

You plunge deeper into dichotomies. You were in the hotel kitchen when you heard the whistling and applause from the shelter. Quickly you went downstairs and found the Palestinian workers all on their feet, chanting the national anthem, 'Abu Ammar' on the TV screen declaring independence. The workers were crying, hugging one another over Yasser Arafat's words. You remember well how there were nude photos everywhere: on the walls, the ceiling, the doors. On the wall were also some Um Kulthum lyrics written in red:

> My love, everything is fate, they say
> Being miserable wasn't our chosen way

That week you went on annual leave. At night you snuck out with other young men in the 'Brigades of Abu Jihad the Martyr' to distribute booklets and posters emblazoned with the text of the Declaration of Independence, the independence that remained on paper. At the same time, some colleagues let you know they were taking annual leave to serve in the army, in the 'zones' to combat the Intifada . . . Your Intifada. What a maze!

How sad the explosion of the place made you. You wanted to go back there and stand up for yourself, for the misfortune of your personal consciousness in this collective merry-go-round—literarily. You wanted an aesthetic victory there, you wanted to develop the scorpion as a character of the novel, you wanted to give him additional features, literary traits. You dare to begin to give him more freedom: instead of going to the mirror, he would run to the stage, stand on his tail, waving some of his legs, his hands. You wanted him to say things maybe you couldn't say yourself, and you planned to train him to entice mirrors. The mirrors were destroyed.

## (13)

## THE SCORPION LEADS A
## GROUP DANCE ON THE MOUNTAIN

Two days ago, I spent the night in front of the parking lot without the appetite to write. I noticed a lot of cars parked in the lot and next to them a huge Bagger excavator taking up a large amount of space, a portion of it covering the place where I usually sit. I was aggravated, but because I didn't feel like writing that night, I avoided picking a fight with anyone, keeping my evil intention within.

Then I said to myself it was just an excavator passing through; maybe the driver had been forced to leave it here due to extenuating circumstances. Usually digger drivers spend the night in them, working mostly at night, at a hundred dollars an hour in this city that had suddenly transformed into a construction site.

Today (3 March 2007), I woke up terribly early and stepped out to see the city getting up: the city's nights are mine; I know them like the back of my hand.

Ramallah is an intelligent city, a lively city, but with this siege, it has started sleeping a little earlier: sharwarma shops are the last to close their doors at around 2 a.m. and the first to wake up are the taxi drivers, who bring vegetable merchants and market employees at 3.30 a.m. to receive their vegetables and prepare their stalls.

A pleasant morning after some rainy days. March's flip-flopping irked me this year. The city yawns.

I looked towards the parking lot, and there was an excavator digging, digging up the parking lot, painfully digging up my memory, my imagination. A shocking scene, my place slowly being murdered, a mere few metres away. I stole another look: the guard's shack (with its stupid red paint) had been moved to the corner; maybe it would become the post of some guard, to put work tools and labourers' clothes, I thought. Two slender young men were affixing, with an air of finality, a huge billboard to a metal base, on it a massive building and a few words of which the largest and clearest said: DUNA SHOPPING CENTRE.

The racket from the digger was appalling. I squeezed my eyes shut in pain and meandered through the city, confused; the world closing in on me, places disappearing from under my feet once more, or rather crashing on my head, reality imposing on the details of my novel, the curse of the plot wringing my neck once more, the place shedding its neutrality, its shards spilling on my head, reaching out its hand to scribble on my manuscript.

I wandered aimlessly. I didn't feel like talking or listening. I felt like I needed to faint, to escape, for even just a few moments from the circle of consciousness—I wanted to run away from myself. I didn't want to hear anything, see anything, say anything; I walked weighed down by disasters and losses, weighed down by meanings. The sound of the giant digger undid me.

The melody of the rebab caught me, a melancholy one at that. I approached the rebab seller, gesturing for him to give me an instrument. I paid the price written on a slip of paper fastened to one of the instruments, 10 dollars.

The rebab seller was stunned when I spoke to him in sign language, his deeply glittering eyes filling with tears. He firmly refused to accept my money, astonished at discovering my seeming deafness and muteness.

I had always wanted to buy a rebab but had kept on postponing it. Whenever I passed by him, I would look at his set-up with evident interest. Catching wind of my attentiveness, he would become more animated, playing while smiling, whereas I would seem moved. Over the long months he grew to recognize me, believing he was communicating with me through his musical notes—so that's why he was stunned; never had I seen such a dumbfounded face.

I realized my utter cruelty, completely unintended, but I couldn't take it back, the bullet had already been shot. I didn't mean to hurt him; I was just in pain and didn't want to say a word. I left him in the same state, deaf and mute, his eyes shining with a profound sadness.

I left for the mountain. I barely spoke with my parents, my sadness shamelessly out in the open and my bout of recklessness undeniable. The day dragged on, my mother preparing everything possible that could come to the mind of an only child. My silence terrified them; they failed to pull me from its clutches. I tried in vain to extricate myself, to reach them.

Seemingly having slept a little just before midnight, I woke up at midnight itself and grabbed my rebab before leaving my room. Right in the middle of the entrance to Mountain Gob, I sat on a rock and played a melody from the heart, which drew out rhythmic lyrics:

*The tattoo became a scorpion*
*Scrambling up glass you can look on*
*He narrates to the whole world*
*A chapter of the story*
*The story of a blond boy*
*Following the thread of the coy*

121

The wadis echoed back the melody and my voice. The cold breezes stung my face and made my legendary hair dance. I played on, the words escaping from my depths:

*From Mountain Gob he came down*
*To an endless ocean*
*He loved the waves*
*Dancing without motivation*

I didn't have a sister, like Saadi at the base of the mountain, to wake people up; I had no sheep thieves around me. I sang of thieves within, I sang of time that had stolen my things, and my places that had hurt me. The melody flowed and gave birth to words:

*The sea, in my dream, I dropped by*
*I asked with the notes of my nai*
*Am I the scorpion?*
*Or is the scorpion me?*

I kept on singing till the end of the night: I sang things and they sang me, I replaced words and they replaced me, I saw plains and mountains before me—as if I were sitting atop a red carpet, and in front was a wall . . . a mirror in which was a young man, thirtyish, his hair smooth and thick, hair of gold, hugging a rebab, singing. Behind me were much whispering and the sound of chairs, tables being moved around.

I kept on singing as if in a dream, seated on a red carpet.

The mirror disappeared and in its place, exactly one step away from me, was a young man, thirtyish, his hair smooth and thick, hair of gold, hugging a rebab, singing:

*Me, am I the mountain, or is the mountain me?*
*Me, am I the sea, or is the sea me?*
*Me, am I the stairs, or are the stairs me?*
*Me, am I the scorpion, or am I a mirror,*
*    or am I a mirror, or am I a mirror?*

I wasn't (he wasn't) simply singing. I was completely like the words chewed up by the mountain, like the jewels tumbling out of the mouth of the girl with plucked-out eyes from one of my aunt's stories.

Across from me, the lights of some cars appeared, rivalling the light of dawn, the sounds of taxi engines transporting a handful of labourers going on their way to the Scorpion Land to work, with permits or by sneaking through the gaps in the wall. The morning began to breathe and I started to feel dew on and all around me. I made out more clearly the tatty mattress my father would sit on during the day, on it a grass-green thin blanket he'd use to cover his body and face whenever someone dropped by to visit. There were small holes of varying sizes in the blanket, its edges blackened by the embers of his cigarettes.

The dew seemed to have roused the smell of tobacco on the blanket and the mattress, pungent Arab tobacco.

He left the house on his crutches, wearing his prosthetic leg, groping his way. I wanted to get up to help him. 'Wait.'

'Stay where you are,' he responded. 'Your scent is guiding me. There's coffee in the thermos, just bring it so we can drink together at Mountain Gob. Your mother prepared it late last night, she barely slept, worried sick about you, and your music flowing throughout the night.'

We sat drinking coffee. I was exhausted, crushed, shattered.

'Listen son, I'm an old man and my "water is on the fire" as they say.'

'I don't understand. How so?'

'When one of us dies, people wash him according to tradition; each person has their portion of water, and mine is on the fire, being warmed up I mean. People no longer heat their water on the fire any more. Things go, but their names remain, son. My end is near is what I'm saying.'

While my father was talking, and while I listened with great difficulty, my head spinning, it occurred to me that dead people don't care if the water is hot or cold. It's absurd to heat up water to wash a dead body. I tried to remain calm, and strung together a sentence after which I wanted to rest rather than hear a response. 'So what if your water is on the fire?'

'My whole life I've been silent, to protect you from becoming an echo to my voice. You know what that means? I've never asked you for anything before, for me, but I'll ask you for something today. Think about marriage, I'm just asking you to think about it.'

For so many years I'd expected him to say something like this to me, but it didn't happen. The answer was in my mind, there. I'd prepared it for a day like this, I didn't know if the same answer was suitable for right now but, because I didn't feel like thinking, and I was beyond exhausted, on the verge of fainting, I plucked the sentence out of my memory and simply changed the number.

The answer was born to the presumed question when I was twenty-five, and my father didn't broach the topic till now, when I'm thirty-five. Ten years ago, I had imagined the scenario, and found a convoluted answer for him: twenty-five years and I've been trying to slip away from your answers to the questions of life, existence, and you want to make me fall into a trap of questions, sons' questions for their fathers? To whom do you want me to bequeath this wandering, this maze? I pulled this answer out, which had always seemed astonishing to me, and simply changed the number.

'Thirty-five years and I've been trying to slip away from your answers to the questions of life, existence, and you want to make me fall into a trap of questions, sons' questions for their fathers? To whom do you want me to bequeath this wandering, this maze?'

'Which questions and answers are you talking about son, why are you putting yourself through such trials? To be a father, you just have to be a father, not a philosopher. Don't underestimate biology. As a man without a leg I know full well, when you touch nothingness, and language can't help you, biology can save you.

'And why are you searching for serious answers to questions that aren't that serious? Sometimes it seems to me that we're lacking the knowledge no less important than the knowledge of life rolling on. Then you want to convince me that your feet haven't started to itch? Aren't you from the family of scratchers?' he asked me jokingly to rescue me from my well of gloom.

I didn't have an answer, or rather simply I didn't want to discuss anything; I thought my answer was staggering, sufficient and conclusive, but it seems it wasn't.

'Everything itches me,' I told him. 'Not just my feet but the whole universe it seems.' I changed the topic. 'Did you read my novel?' My mother had taken the bag with my manuscript in the afternoon, and I forgot that I had decided no one should read it till I was done.

'You mean how many times have we read it? We spent the night, your mother reading aloud and me listening, reliving your life through a thousand details that we'd never get fed up of reading.'

My father had responded with such enthusiasm; maybe he had wanted to revive me from my rapid burnout, betrayed by my tone. I had asked not to hear the answer but to ask him a question whose answer I wished he'd stretch out forever. I feel my senses leaving me and I don't want to amputate my conversation with my father—it's enough that his leg is amputated; I don't want to hurt him, it's enough that I hurt the rebab seller today.

'Did you like the novel?'

'Did I! It enchanted me, duped me. More than once I wanted to get up and walk on my two feet, more than once I felt the emptiness of my missing leg was just an illusion.' He glanced around, his grave tone and melancholy features transforming to jubilance. 'Actually, more than once I wanted to get up and impregnate your mother!'

Was her womb forlorn or his testicles? I wondered.

'For a long time I didn't read,' he said. 'Then I was an insatiable reader. When by nature you're a thoughtful reader, and you lose a leg, you feel maybe no one will ever be able to add anything to you. I read you and you added something to me. But listen here, yes, I lost my leg, but I don't want you to lose your foothold. I lost my leg but what's more painful is that it looks like you've lost your way.'

My mother made her way out towards us. Shocked at seeing my face dark, and inflamed (something my blind father couldn't have noticed), she stretched out her palm to my forehead.

'Fire, fire! Your body's burning up darling!' Quickly she fetched compresses and a large red basin she plunged my feet into. She began to apply the compresses to my head while I shivered, it seems that the fever was why I was in pieces, without realizing it.

'I wanted to bring you inside last night but your father said, "Let him play." Looks like you fell ill.'

Water, so much water under my feet. So much water.

'How did you drag the sea here, Mama? How did you bring it here?'

'You're ill. I'm going to call the doctor.'

'No, no, it's just my legs are slipping on the mirrors, my legs are slipping. I'm scrambling and they slip. Why these stairs? Salty water in my mouth, sea water is salty.'

'The boy's sweating, he's dripping sweat, do something dear! What a pity! If only you could. . . .'

'How did you get here, Baba, to the Mediterranean shores? How did you come down from the mountain? Is the Mediterranean water salty? My sweat? What are you doing here?'

'Wash my feet in the water, wash my feet, and wash the foot of my amputated leg in the water of the Mediterranean. Go on, rub it well. My foot's itching, rub between the toes, the toes, rub well between the toes.'

\*

A scientific detail that the narrator can't ignore: scorpions don't drink water and they don't have pores, so they can't sweat or be dripping with sweat.